Pleasuring the Pinkerton

formerly Taming Talia

Loving the Lawman 2

Marie-Nicole Ryan

RYANDALE PUBLISHING

PLEASURING THE PINKERTON,
formerly published as TAMING TALIA

1st print publication, March 2017, Ryandale Publishing
2nd print publication, July 2019

ISBN-

Published in the United States of America
Library of Congress registration number: TX 7-794-861

Chapter One

Rot in peace.

Natalia Salacito Montrose stood over her husband's grave with a clenched jaw and reined in the urge to spit. She clutched a clump of earth for an indeterminate length of time, then opened her fingers and let the dirt fall, each granule a symbol of her newfound freedom. Across the arroyo, a breeze whipped up and blew the dirt in a fine spray over the top of his casket. Served the bastard right he was buried in a plain pine box.

Rot in peace.

And the sooner the better.

"That's that, then." She smiled at the preacher. His watery eyes widened. His lips moved as if to speak but stopped. Perhaps he thought, *better not.*

"I'm returning to the ranch." She glared at the onlookers gathered around the grave and dared them to speak. "I prefer to grieve in private." There, let them talk about her inhospitable attitude. Brushing the dirt from her hands, she held her head high, gathered her black skirts and swept to the waiting buggy.

Ignoring the raised eyebrows and open mouths of the few who attended the burial was easy. She'd tolerated her husband's Anglo acquaintances the entire eight years of their marriage. Enough of their insincere condolences. It wasn't as if her late husband had been taken by a sudden illness or accident. Oh no. He'd died in a gambling-house brawl—at least by the sheriff's report. He'd been too polite to tell her anything else.

Others weren't so circumspect and had cheerfully informed her that *after* the argument was over, her husband had taken himself upstairs to enjoy the favors of one of the soiled doves. His dalliance was interrupted by a knife in the back, courtesy of the man with whom he'd argued.

Who cared? None of the so-called fine folks who deigned to attend the burial. And certainly not his wife. The bastard was out of her life for good. All she had to do was run the ranch and enjoy her good fortune. As a wealthy widow, she was bound to have plenty of eligible suitors, but for now, all she wanted was a real man between her thighs. Any man would do. As long as he was clean. A man to ride hard until she relieved all the frustrations and longings of the last eight years.

"Home." She nodded at the ranch foreman, took his offered hand and climbed into the buggy. Too bad he was closer to fifty than thirty. Clean enough, but she doubted he could give her the kind of ride she desperately needed.

As the foreman turned the buggy northward, the sun sank low in the sky, leaving the flat-topped Rabbit Ear Mountains to cast their stunted shadows over what had been a glorious October day. In the distance, she spied a lone horseman who had just turned south toward La Mesa. Behind him lay the ever-present mountains which one of her early teachers taught were the remnants of ancient volcanoes.

Her mouth tugged into a smile. A perfect stranger. Someone headed south who was passing through and would never be seen again. What were the chances?

Shading his eyes from the sun's glare, Jared Fields stood in the stirrups and peered into the distance. Behind him were two flat-topped humps, the Rabbit Ear Mountains, marking the spot where the Santa Fe Trail branched into the Cimarron Cutoff. His destination of La Mesa, located in the northeast corner of the New Mexico Territory, lay a short ride to the south.

Not much longer. His ass ached from days in the saddle. Couldn't complain, though. Considering the dismal conclusion to his Texas assignment, it was his good fortune to be in the right area and available for another. One more chance to prove himself and earn his keep.

Since he was Pinkerton's closest agent, he'd been dispatched to La Mesa. His new client, the wealthy and prominent George Montrose of New York City, was convinced his son's wife had engineered his murder in order to inherit his fortune and vast New Mexico landholdings. Jared's mission was to prove Montrose's suspicions correct. If he found otherwise, his assignment was to bring the widow, and thereby control of his son's estate and any possible heirs, back to New York City.

No doubt discovering the truth would prove a simple task, unlike his last assignment. A few questions here and there would get to the bottom of the issue soon enough. Should the widow need convincing, he possessed the means of encouraging her. What woman in her right mind would hesitate to leave this vast and desolate area of New Mexico in the dust and make her way to New York? It was the center of the civilized and cultured world—at least as far as upper-class New Yorkers were concerned.

While New York had been the center of his world for most of his youth, he'd never realized the breadth and sheer beauty the West offered a man who needed a new life. And he'd definitely needed a new start after being disowned. When a friend suggested he join the Pinkerton Agency, Jared had jumped at the chance. The agency offered him freedom as much as it had given him a purpose in life. His background made him the perfect agent for the more delicate assignments, where his manners and breeding distinguished him from their common agents. Pinkerton agents were feared, and rightly so. Private lawmen, some called them. Others, renegades and thugs.

Here in the wide-open plains, he had a free hand in dealing with unforeseen problems and needed only a telegraph office to make his reports and receive assignments. So what if it wasn't the life he'd been groomed for by his father? It was Jared's life on his own terms, and no one needed to know or care what a disappointment he was.

*

Hours after her husband's funeral, Natalia slammed the door to Reginald's bedchamber and strode over to his chifforobe. She jerked open the doors, ready to haul out her late husband's clothes and toss them onto his bed. Now that he was out of her life for good, she would instruct Sarita to burn them. A bonfire was all they were good for.

No, that would be wasteful. Better they be distributed to the needy.

Shutting the wardrobe door, she returned to her bedchamber. It was comfortable, though slightly spartan. Nothing like Reginald's massive mahogany furniture from New York City.

The four posts of her bed were hewn from the local mesquite, with iron spindles joining the head and footboards. A simple but colorful counterpane covered the thick feather mattress. Her bed was certainly big enough for two, but most nights she slept alone and undisturbed.

A traditional curved fireplace occupied one corner of the room, while a tall oak chifforobe sat in the other corner. A one-armed horsehair settee sat at an angle to catch the best daylight for reading. Reginald insisted on calling the piece of furniture by its French name, a tongue-twisting—for her at least—*chaise longue*. A small dressing table occupied the area next to the window.

On the table rested a silver-backed brush and mirror—gifts from a mother she'd barely known—and a bottle of expensive French scent, Reginald's only gift. Picking it up, she removed the stopper, sniffed and wrinkled her nose. She set it back; she'd never cared for the stuff. At least the crystal bottle was pretty. The cut glass acted as a prism capturing rays of sunlight which washed the walls with glittering shapes of color.

She stripped from her widow's weeds, allowing the silk garments to drop the floor. She reached around and loosened the laces of her corset. In the chifforobe's mirror, she caught sight of her body, the body Reginald never gazed at adoringly or with the least bit of desire. No, he'd rather waste his time gambling and whoring at the Silver Queen than be husband to his wife.

Other than taking her roughly from behind, he never touched her with love. Never kissed her. Never stroked her body like the fine instrument it was.

She moved her hands up and down her figure, jutting her breasts. *Just look at what he missed.* She tweaked her nipples and imagined a man's mouth suckling them. Her core thrummed with the need for release. She rolled down her pantaloons—stupid things—and stepped out of them. A triangle of black curls beckoned her to explore the damp folds. True, he'd taken her virginity, but he'd never given her pleasure a second thought. Only his own.

Still standing in front of the mirror, she found the nub hidden in the damp folds of her cleft. With one hand she caressed her breast while she circled the nubbin with the fingers of her other, increasing the pressure until her thighs trembled and her pussy grew slick and damp. Her breathing quickened. Her skin grew warm. When her knees began to tremble, she stumbled to the bed, sinking into the soft feather mattress. Her body heated, and she came quickly with a rush of pleasure.

Lying back on the bed, she caught her breath and marveled how easily she could give herself more pleasure in a few seconds than her late husband had in eight years of what had amounted to a prison sentence.

Thankfully not a life sentence after all.

Chapter Two

Jared sat at the bar of the Silver Queen. It was as dismal as most saloons he'd run across in the New Mexico Territory, replete with the smell of stale beer, sweat and spilled whiskey. He signaled the barkeep. "Whiskey." He slugged down a shot and regretted it immediately. A fiery burn scorched the back of his throat, ripping all the way down his gullet.

Damn.

Was it too much to ask that this one-horse cow town have a decent whiskey, or at least one that wouldn't threaten to dissolve a man's innards with every swallow?

Four men sat in a corner playing poker, while a half-dressed whore flaunted her wares over the shoulder of one of the cowhands. Another whore sidled up to Jared, smelling of flowery perfume and sweat. "Not now, honey," he said. Not now and not that desperate. She flounced off with a huff, setting her sights on another of the card players.

In town for two days, he'd kept his ear to the ground. Many of La Mesa's good citizens were more than happy to repeat the latest gossip about the object of his quest,

Natalia Montrose. Seems the inhabitants of La Mesa were of two minds about the lady. A good many, who seemed to have known her all her life, felt sorry for her loss and believed she deserved her good fortune. Even the local sheriff, a no-nonsense man by the name of Moulton, counted himself in that group. The lawman went so far as to say Jared was wasting his time pursuing the widow. Montrose had been killed in a whore's bed by the man who'd earlier called Montrose out as a cheat.

A few others in town thought she was a jumped-up, gold-digging Mexican hussy who had her husband murdered for his fortune. Likely the truth lay somewhere between, although her late husband's father certainly believed her responsible.

A whiff of horse and even more regrettable body odor wafted his way. "Stranger, you looking for work?"

Jared turned and examined the miscreant standing at his side. The man was short and stocky, too covered in trail dust to determine his complexion or hair color. One of his muddy brown eyes gazed directly, while the other stared at the wall.

Focusing on the straight eye, Jared leaned back with his elbows on the bar. "Depends on what it is and how long it might take."

"Need hands for a trail drive. Herd's rounded up, but one of the cowhands broke his leg, and we be already shorthanded. We got coupla thousand head rounded up ready to ship to Fort Sumpter and Fort Roswell."

Granted the man only had one good eye, but what made him think Jared looked like a cowhand? He straightened his string tie and brushed a speck of dust from his jacket.

"Afraid I must decline. Not so fond of cattle."

The cowboy snorted. "Figured as much. Appears more like you be handy with cards."

"Been known to play a hand or two." Or ten. Or twenty. Weren't cards the reason his father disowned him nearly fifteen years ago?

"How's about you and me plays a hand?" The cowboy sniffed and wiped his nose with a grimy cuff. "I win, and you sign on."

"Why would I risk doing that? I'm not much on following orders. Rather give 'em."

The cowboy shook his head. "Poor Missus Montrose. She's a widow woman now her man's got hisself killed. She's gonna need the money driving those cattle to market will bring."

"Montrose? Yes, heard about him." Jared glanced toward the stairs leading to the whores' rooms.

"Yessir. That's right. Died right upstairs, he did."

"You don't say." Hell, yes, he was interested. Just not in the cattle drive.

"Still could use some help, if you've a mind to."

Jared nodded, smiled and picked up his hat from the bar. "Name's Fields. I'm at the hotel, and I'll think about it." He raised a brow. "Your name?"

"Moose Foulkes—that's 'cause they say I smell worse'n a moose." No arguing that salient fact. "Where you from, Fields?"

"St. Louis," Jared lied without a blink. Lies came easily to Pinkerton agents, part of their stock in trade. "Nice little town you have here. Might even settle down."

Not for all the money in New York City.

*

Later that same day, after receiving directions to the Montrose spread from the sheriff, Jared dropped in at the telegraph office, which also served as the post office, to telegraph his employers with his next move.

Two or three miles from town, Jared rode up to a spreading hacienda-style house with a red-tiled roof. A long porch covered the entrance, multiple rounded arches with supports painted in a bright blue. He'd seen bigger haciendas in California and farther south, but still, the long adobe dwelling was an impressive sight. Well-kept, it was already well-lit against the coming of night by two large wrought-iron lanterns with sides of wavy glass to keep the desert breezes from extinguishing the candles. Each lantern hung on either side of massive, carved double doors.

Jared pulled up his collar against the cold, looking forward to getting inside. When he'd started his short journey to the hacienda, the sun had been shining, but now storm clouds were building in the northeast, accompanied by a biting wind that nearly blew off his Stetson.

Uncertain of his reception, he slowed his horse and readied to dismount when a cowboy appeared and planted himself at the animal's head. He stared up at Jared. "How can I help ya, mister?"

"Jared Fields to see Mrs. Montrose to pay my condolences and speak to her regarding a private business matter."

The cowhand shrugged. "Don't know if she's seeing visitors, but if she is, she's inside."

Swinging his leg over Midnight's back, Jared dismounted and handed the reins to the cowboy. "See he's rubbed down and watered. Some feed wouldn't be amiss." Giving orders came easily. He'd grown up tripping over servants.

"Sure thing."

"Thank you." Already looking forward to meeting the Widow Montrose, Jared didn't look back. He raised the heavy wrought-iron ring that served as a door knocker and let it fall on the ornate door. He waited. The door was quickly opened by a maid of obvious Spanish blood. She was dressed in black with white cuffs and a silver necklace with a turquoise stone pendant.

"Mr. Fields to see Mrs. Montrose."

"The *señora* isn't seeing anyone..." she said, her assessing gaze traveling up and down his frame. "But maybe she will make an exception, just this once." She nodded and gestured for him to follow. She led him to a sitting room with a fireplace. "I will tell the *señora* you're here."

Thankful for the heat from the flames, he stood in front of the fireplace. Reginald Montrose hadn't spared any expense in outfitting the old hacienda to his sophisticated Eastern tastes, at least in this room. Fine furniture from the East, or maybe even England, filled the drawing room.

Waiting for the arrival of Montrose's widow, he kept his back to the door. Would he find her as comely as he'd been told? Beautiful women might be plentiful in the cities, but what passed for beauty in New Mexico Territory remained to be seen. Frankly, he couldn't blame the woman for marrying a rich Easterner.

Rich or poor, all the women he'd ever known desired to make a good marriage. The friends of his youth joked that having a pretty wife never hurt, but a pretty and rich wife was even better. As for him, he'd enjoyed his share of beautiful, rich women, but preferred his freedom to a ball and chain.

Deep in thought, Natalia glanced through the ranch's ledgers spread before her on the desk. Now that she was mistress of her own domain, she had time to consider how to spend her days. Before Reginald lost his miserable life in the Silver Queen, she'd been a lady of forced leisure. Controlling bastard wouldn't even allow her to ride without an escort. Born and bred in the area, she knew the land as well as anyone around. And could outride any man.

She hated embroidery, quilting and calling on the few Anglo wives who braved the trip westward. La Mesa society was limited and stiff—at least Reginald's version. Those of Spanish heritage didn't usually mix with Anglos. What she'd ever seen in Reginald, she couldn't remember. Not that her father had ever given her a choice. True, Reginald had been distinguished, polished, and *seemed* a gentleman. But what he'd seen in her was no mystery.

The land. Yes, he'd wanted her father's land. Between the two of them, they brokered a deal—a deal that included her hand in marriage and an enormous amount of gold and silver in her father's pocket.

Her wily father got the better end of the deal. Nothing new about that. But now that someone had done her the unexpected favor of killing her husband, the land and cattle were hers. And she wasn't about to give them back to her father or anyone else. Making the ranch thrive and running it as a successful business were now more important than ever.

Sarita entered the sitting room and cleared her throat. "Someone to see you, *señora*."

"I'm not seeing callers." Natalia held back her exasperation, keeping her tone soft. There'd been enough shouting at servants while her husband was alive. She had no intention of continuing his rude manners.

"He say not social." The housekeeper's dark eyes sparkled with excitement. "Very nice-looking man. Dressed in black."

Natalia wrinkled her nose. "The *padre*? I had enough of him at the service. Tell him I'm indisposed."

A quick shake of the housekeeper's head set her starched white cap to bobbing. "Most definitely *not* a preacher man."

"You said 'nice looking'?"

"*Muy* handsome. *Sí.*"

Good old Reginald had forbidden any of the house servants from using their native language, but that was only one of the many changes she planned. She smiled. After all, it was her native language too. "I'll see him. Show him to the front parlor." She nodded at the housekeeper. "And since he's *muy* handsome, serve us some coffee." Maybe Natalia would do more than *see* him.

She waited until Sarita left the room, then walked over to an ornate gold-framed looking glass and surveyed her appearance with an arched brow.

Excellent. More than good enough for the man in black.

Composing her emotions, she walked down the central hall to the front parlor, where a fire had already been laid to ward off the chill of the late October evening. She found a tall, lean man, dressed in black as the housekeeper had said, standing in front of the fireplace, his back to her.

"You wish to see me? *Señor—*"

He turned and smiled, his well-trimmed dark mustache quirking to one side. His square jaw was clean-shaven, and he smelled of spicy Bay Rum, denoting a very recent visit to the barber. His dark brows shot up, his pale gray eyes glittering with obvious interest.

"Fields, Jared Fields, at your service." His voice was low and possessed a cultured tone.

Madre de Dios. Sarita was right. *Muy* handsome indeed. Tall, lean, clean and saddle-hardened—just what a frustrated widow needed. What *could* he want?

"*Señor* Fields, how may I help you?" His accent and manner weren't those of a *Californio* or a common cowboy. Maybe he was someone who'd known her husband before he came west. If so, she didn't trust his coming here. Not now. She had too much to lose.

"I met one of your hands today. Said you needed someone for a cattle drive."

Disappointment stabbed through her. A *vaquero* after all. "Then see my foreman." The sharp retort escaped before she could call it back. Ready to sweep from the room, she picked up her skirts but was stopped short by the sound of his voice.

"Hear me out. Your hand, a Mr. Foulkes, also mentioned you were running the ranch alone."

She halted, glancing over her shoulder at the tall

stranger. "I already have a foreman." *Dios*, but he was a choice specimen of manhood. He held a black Stetson in his hands, and a half grin occupied his lean, tanned face. What did *he* have to be amused about?

"Madam, if you would allow me to say my piece..." His dark, raven's wing brows elevated as he awaited her answer.

She let out a small sigh and faced her visitor. "Go ahead, then." She took a deep breath, knowing the act would cause her breasts to jut and capture his attention. If only he would stop talking.

His gaze flickered from her face. "It wasn't my intention to hire on as one of your hands. It comes to me that you might need my advice—financial advice, that is. I'm from St. Louis and built up a successful firm which does just that. *Did,* I should clarify. I sold my half of the business to my partner and came westward. On my arrival in this fair— uh, city, it came to my attention that as a new widow of substantial holdings, you might have need of such advice."

"I see." In spite of his elegant manners, Mr. Fields was more interested in her money and land than her body. What was it with men and money? She drew up, gathering her most imperious and fiery manner. "Mr. Fields, do I appear as if I was born last night? It comes to my mind that perhaps you are a confidence man who, rather than advise me, would take advantage of what you suppose is my ignorance."

Her handsome visitor's eyes widened, and his back straightened. "To the contrary, it's obvious to me, and should be to anyone, that you are an exceptional woman of perspicacity, and as such I would advise you to telegraph my former business partner in St. Louis to check my references. Perhaps doing so would convince you of my good faith." He nodded, but still a smirk played about his mouth.

"And perhaps I don't require your services at all." *At least not those.* "I'm quite capable of managing my late husband's holdings."

"Madam, your late husband's holdings lie far beyond this ranch."

"Is that so?" Raising her chin a notch, she took a step toward him, each of her hands clenching a fistful of silk skirts. "And how do you come by your knowledge of my late husband's affairs?"

Who was he really? Most assuredly an opportunist, at the very least. Possibly someone sent by Reginald's family.

Not that either scenario precluded her using him for her own amusement.

"The town weekly, the *La Mesa Messenger*, I believe it's called, devoted several columns to his"—her visitor paused and cleared his throat—"death and history."

Natalia's cheeks burned. "Yes, the weekly rag was quite generous with its coverage." As if everyone within ten miles wasn't already aware of the humiliating details. Gossip spread faster in La Mesa than wildfire on the prairie. And yet standing so near to this virile and handsome man had her heart fluttering. Heat suffused her cheeks. Could he tell she was so moved by his presence?

Eager to change the subject, she walked to the settee and sat. "Where are my manners? Please be seated, Mr. Fields." She gestured to a straight-backed oak chair.

Her visitor nodded and sat across from her.

Sarita arrived with a tray and set it on the sideboard, then withdrew. Ah, her housekeeper and friend had impeccable timing. Natalia rose and walked to the sideboard, then glanced over her shoulder at her visitor. "How do you take your coffee? Or would you prefer tea?"

"Black. Coffee is fine, Mrs. Montrose."

"I thought as much. Most men seem to prefer it that way," she offered with a smile. After adding sugar to her coffee, she picked up both cups of the steaming, fragrant brew and handed one to her visitor. She sat and sipped. The sugar cut the bite of the strong coffee Sarita made a habit of brewing.

Natalia cradled the cup in her hands, relishing the warmth. "Why are you really here, Mr. Fields? La Mesa is a small town. Surely you could find more lucrative business opportunities farther west in, say...San Francisco. Or maybe you're chasing gold or silver? Is that it—did you journey west for adventure or to seek your fortune?"

"It's true I'm of a mind to see San Francisco, but I also wanted to see this wide and wonderful country of ours."

"Yes, a good bit of it used to belong to *my* people...and not so very long ago."

He nodded in her direction, a smile playing across his lips. "*You've* done very well..."

"Done very well?" Her breath caught in her throat. This tall, elegant man sitting before her had no idea what Reginald had put her through. Who was he to judge?

"You have a comfortable situation here. Land, cattle, and no doubt a good deal of money to invest."

"Ah, back again to my *money*." She tamped down her irritation and averted her gaze shyly. "And here I hoped your interest might be more...personal."

His brows shot up, but his gray gaze grew warm, and one corner of his mouth twisted upward in a grin. "Alas, I would never presume, as I am only too cognizant of your recent loss."

Presume indeed? His very tone mocked her, even as his words were faultlessly respectful.

"Where are you from, Mr. Fields?"

"St. Louis, as I said earlier."

"No, I don't hear the Midwestern twang. Your manner of speaking sounds more like that of one from the northeast."

He sipped from his cup, then nodded. "You've caught me out. I was born and reared in New York City, but I left home as a young man. Tried my hand at various enterprises before I settled and found success in St. Louis."

"As a young man. Surely not so long ago?"

"I was twenty when I left New York. That was three and ten years ago, Mrs. Montrose."

Thirty-three years to her thirty. True, marriage to Reginald had saved her from the stigma of being an unmarried woman and a burden to her family. Not that she cared, but the lure of Reginald's gold had proved too much for her father to resist. Perhaps it was his plan all along that she would outlive Reginald and the land would return to their family, along with all of her late husband's wealth.

Small price to pay if his only daughter were trapped in a loveless marriage.

Small price indeed. Two could play that game.

Snapping from her reverie, she smiled. "So you are an adventurer?" Fixing her gaze on his expressive mouth and thick mustache, she continued, "Or perhaps you were disinherited?"

He blinked, as if startled, then laughed, a hearty rumble that warmed her. "I assure you, I wasn't disowned for any sins of youth, if that's what you're thinking, Mrs. Montrose. I discovered quite young I craved adventure beyond the confines of my family's banking business."

"And yet in St. Louis, you ended up advising others on financial matters. Not so far from the confines of your youth, was it?" Her forefinger circled the rim of her coffee cup as she watched his sensual mouth. Was his mustache stiff and bristly or soft? Would it tickle? Her breathing grew rapid, her cheeks warming as she imagined him crushing her lips with his. Desire gathered in her lower belly and heat pooled between her legs.

"No, indeed. When the financial world of St. Louis began to pall, my thirst for new horizons reasserted itself."

Her gaze flitted from his mouth to his warm gray gaze. She worried her bottom lip before responding with a teasing smile. "But yet once again, you are here offering to advise me in such matters."

This time he chuckled. Such a good-humored man, whether he was an opportunist or no. "Seems like I cannot get away from what I am," he said, gazing over his coffee cup in the most speculative manner.

"Indeed." Natalia sipped from her cup, then set it down. "Would you care to stay for dinner? It will be but a simple repast, but I hope you'll find it satisfactory."

"You're too gracious. I accept." A single brow arched. "And after dinner?"

"I would be inclined to hear what you propose...in

regards to my finances." The last she added quickly, lest he intuit her purpose.

His steely gaze raked from her face to her breasts and then back to her face. "I would be delighted to clarify my proposition...to our mutual benefit, of course."

"Of course."

Suddenly the mesquite wood fire popped, causing Natalia to gasp with surprise. Her visitor smiled, his gaze warm. "Mesquite burns hot."

"*Sí*, mesquite is a hard wood," she said with a flutter of her lashes. "Indeed, it burns long and hot."

Her visitor shot her a questioning glance and cleared his throat. His Adam's apple bobbed once with his quick swallow. "And fragrant. During part of my journey westward, I traveled with a wagon train. Any meat cooked over the mesquite was left with a rich and unaccustomed smoky flavor. I enjoyed it greatly. I assure you there's nothing like it in New York or St. Louis."

"I'm sure you will find there are many flavors here in New Mexico to which you are probably unaccustomed."

"Indeed, I look forward to discovering *many* of them while I'm here."

His pale gaze bore into her, as if reading her every intention. Her breath caught, and her mouth grew dry. She tried to swallow.

The housekeeper cleared her throat. "Dinner is ready, *señora.*"

More than grateful for the interruption, Natalia started, quickly recovered, then rose from the settee. Sarita's arrival was again timely. However she managed the feat, Natalia often suspected the woman of listening at the door. Not that it mattered.

"If you'll follow me..." She nodded toward the central hall.

He proffered his arm. "If you'll allow me."

She smiled up at him and placed her hand lightly on his muscled forearm. "You're very kind, Mr. Fields."

As much as her late husband insisted on running an Eastern-style household, they seldom stood on ceremony unless he had company, especially if it was someone he wanted to impress. In other words, he didn't waste his citified manners on his wife. Yet, with no one around to observe, Mr. Field's polite offering of his arm greatly pleased her. However, his elegant manners were likely a front for more sinister intentions. He hadn't exactly tried to hide his sharp interest in her finances, had he? Perhaps by keeping him at arm's length, she could divine his true purpose.

Pretty words and fine manners were cheap enough.

Chapter Three

With the Widow Montrose's hand resting lightly on his arm, Jared clenched his jaw. Never had the mere touch of a woman's hand on his forearm caused such a rush of lust. Imagine what feelings her touching his cock would engender. Doubtless he'd been on the trail too long and without the comfort of a woman.

Instead, he concentrated on his surroundings. The dining room table was generously lit by beeswax candles, not a smoky kerosene lamp. Another fireplace occupied the far corner of the spacious room. Montrose must've had the carved mahogany table and chairs brought from back East. Indeed, they were quite similar to the ones where Jared had grown up in his father's home. An unaccustomed wave of homesickness swept over him, shaking him.

He recalled the last argument with his father. Couldn't blame the old man for kicking him out. He'd deserved it.

The widow's soft voice brought him back to the present. "Mr. Fields, I hope you like beef stew. I warned you it would be a simple meal. Since my husband's untimely passing, I frequently eat in the kitchen with my housekeeper. It's comfortable and not so lonely."

"Beef stew is an admirable dish, especially in the fall. But you eat in the kitchen with your servants?"

"There's only my housekeeper. She's known me since I was a child and knows what I like. My late husband hired what he called a *real cook* from New York City." The corner of her mouth lifted in a slight smile. "However, you're a little late for her fancy fare. I'm afraid she left on the stage before the funeral."

"Before the funeral?"

"Yes, we didn't get on." Lips pursed, her beautiful oval face pulled into a frown. "I can only guess the reasons, but they might have something to do with the color of my skin. Or possibly the moon eyes she made at my husband."

Had Montrose been unfaithful with his cook too? Right under his wife's nose? What man in his right mind would cheat with a wife like this at his side? What a beauty Natalia Montrose was, with the blackest of hair and darkest of eyes. Eyes that sparkled with humor and intelligence. Eyes that challenged him to take her. And burnished skin that begged for his touch.

Or did he have it wrong? Was her desire all in his mind?

To his way of thinking, she certainly had a reason or two to want Montrose out of the way.

Hold on. He wasn't here to absolve or justify the murder of his client's son. His assignment was to find the truth.

After he seated her at the head of the table, she gestured to her right, where there was a second place setting of simple stoneware. "I don't believe in a great deal of formality, Mr. Fields. I had quite enough of it the eight years I was married." She unfolded a linen napkin and placed it in her lap.

The housekeeper brought in a large tureen, then ladled a generous portion into his bowl and a smaller portion into her mistress's bowl. The rich, beefy fragrance wafted upward to his nostrils, causing his stomach to growl. "Smells wonderful."

"I caution you, it might be spicier than what you're used to. Sarita has quite a way with herbs and seasonings."

The housekeeper returned with a platter of flatbread and a covered stoneware bowl of butter, then set them on the table.

Natalia nodded her approval. "Would you like more coffee, Mr. Fields, or perhaps some red wine? My late husband kept a wine cellar with a variety of vintages. A Spanish Rioja would go well with the stew."

As much as he would have loved a rich red to go along with the hearty stew, he couldn't risk losing focus. Not with the heady beauty on his left. He shook his head. "Coffee will be fine."

His hostess took her first bite of the stew and savored it by letting out a small, "Mm." She smiled. "Don't be afraid of the spiciness. A bit of heat only adds to the enjoyment." She broke a piece of flatbread in half and slathered it with butter from the crock. She ate it, then slowly licked the butter from her lips.

Good God. Her words were simple enough, but the throaty undertone in her voice led him to think of more than food. As for the manner with which she took pleasure in her food, that only made him think of other earthier pleasures.

Mouth dry, he swallowed hard, then speared a piece of beef. After swallowing, he said, "You're right about the spice. It's delicious. I've never tasted anything like it." He quickly followed with a buttered bite of the flatbread. Cornbread, but not sweet like the johnnycake of his childhood.

The sweetness and sensual texture of the creamy butter made a perfect complement to the peppery stew. Too many meals of dried jerky had deadened his appetite, which was now fully awake. As were all his appetites. He held back on the desire to shovel in the stew like a cowhand on the trail, for the situation called for his best manners.

The light from the candles sparkled in the widow's eyes. She watched him carefully between ladylike bites, quickly dropping her gaze when he held hers too long. The lady seemed to be playing an odd game of flirtation mixed with a measure of deviousness.

"Now tell me, Mr. Fields, how would *you* manage my holdings?" Again, an underlying note of challenge in her tone.

Stalling for time, he sipped his coffee. "First, I would go over all of your late husband's financial records and holdings to assure everything was in order."

"And if something were out of order? How would you know?" She smiled, reaching for her coffee. She sipped daintily, then licked her full upper lip ever so slightly.

God, what a mouth she had. A mouth meant for kissing... He could only imagine her full lips around his cock.

"Mr. Fields?" An underlying note of amusement.

Damn. Try as he might, he couldn't remember the last time he'd had a woman. "Sorry, I'm afraid my train of thought wandered." She *was* playing him. Surely she knew beauty like hers would leave most men—even this man—panting like dogs to bed her.

He cleared his throat. "As to your question, how would I know? I would organize the available paperwork. Bills of sale. Land deeds. Mineral holdings. Bank statements. Stock certificates and earnings. It would all fall into place quite logically, I assure you."

"And then?"

"I would look into everyday expenses for maintaining this ranch. If you desired to rid yourself of what is likely an enormous expense, running an estate of this size, I could set up an auction. You might want to consider relocating to San Francisco or even the northeast."

"The northeast?" As she rose from her chair, the widow's eyes flashed with anger. "Leave the land where I grew up? Leave the land which is part of my soul?" She slapped her hand on the table. "Never!"

The woman had fire in her eyes, and, where her home was concerned, a fire in her belly. Whether she possessed this same fire in bed, he desired to know more than anything.

But first he must know whether or not she had his client's son murdered.

"The land," she said. "This place is everything to me. It was taken from my family not once, but twice. I won't part with it for any reason."

"Twice?"

"Yes, twice." She strode about the room, waving her hands in the air. "Once when the area came under control of the United States. My family had enough hidden gold and influence in the area that they managed to buy it back piece by piece, nearly bankrupting themselves over the years. Then a second time when my father traded me and the land in one tidy parcel in return for my husband's newfound gold. My father and anyone else will play hell getting this land back. It belongs to *me* and will belong to my heirs. But my merciless, mercenary father will never see a square single inch of this land back under his control...ever."

"Heirs? Did your husband leave you...?"

"No, damn him! He couldn't quite manage that feat either."

Fury was written across her face, but before he could make any response, her housekeeper entered, clearing her throat. "Pardon, but the last two men are ready to leave before the weather gets any worse. They want to know if you have any further instructions."

The housekeeper's diversion seemed to calm the widow somewhat. She gave a polite nod. "I'll just be a moment," she said, then swept from the room as elegantly as any society dame back home.

There was no doubt about it. The woman was a handful. The more he talked with her, the more he realized he had little chance of succeeding in his assignment. Even if he proved the widow had nothing to do with Montrose's death, there was no way she would leave New Mexico of her own volition. The very idea of attempting to drag her kicking and screaming for two and a half thousand miles to New York City was daunting, to say the least.

He shut his eyes and pinched the bridge of his nose. Alerted by quick, light footsteps on the tile floor and the swishing of silk skirts, he heard her before he saw her. He looked over his shoulder. The widow had returned.

Her cheeks flushing, she glided to the chair on his left, then sat. "Please accept my apology, Mr. Fields. My behavior was unforgivably rude. This land—my land—is something I am very passionate about."

"I've always admired passion in a lady, Mrs. Montrose. The apology is mine to make." He rose from his chair, and, taking her hand in his, he bowed. "You have suffered a loss. I should have waited for a more appropriate time to call with my proposition. With your permission, I'll take my leave and return at a later date."

She jerked her hand away. "No!" The widow's jaw clenched, and one hand went to her throat, where she toyed with an ivory broach. "I mean—the rudeness is on my part, not yours. And I'm *most* interested in hearing what you have to say about my finances. My position is difficult." She covered his hand with her delicate one, entreating him to remain. "I don't trust my husband's local associates or his family in the East. And I certainly don't trust my father to look after my interests. I have no one I can trust. You—you are a stranger and therefore can remain neutral."

His plan to insinuate himself into the lovely widow's good graces was working, but why didn't it please him more? Frankly, he felt guilty. The woman before him was nothing like the insipid society beauties he'd known at home. Too bad he was here to prove she'd murdered her husband. Seeing her fire when confronted with the idea of selling her vast land holdings, he could easily believe she'd ordered the deed without a qualm. And from what he'd heard in town about Reginald Montrose, he was perhaps a man who needed killing.

No one had been arrested for Montrose's death. According to the sheriff, Montrose had been in the midst of fornicating with a whore when he was attacked. His attacker, a drifter by the name of Juan Ojeda, had fled the scene. And his escape was suspicious because he'd gotten away without a trace.

"You're so quiet. Will you help me?" The entreaty in her tone, the underlying intensity, the unspoken need in her eyes—what man could refuse?

Not this man.

He swallowed, then nodded. "Yes, Mrs. Montrose, I will."

"Good." She smiled, her dark eyes glowing and lashes fluttering at his response. "Since we are to be in business of a sorts together, you must you call me Natalia. I don't care to be reminded of *his* surname at every turn."

"I wouldn't presume to be so familiar." What a liar. If he wasn't careful, they would be more than *familiar*.

She peered at him from eyes as dark as a moonless night, a slight smile curving her full red lips. "I insist. And I shall call you Jared," she said, following her bold statement with an emphatic nod.

How was it she made the sound of his name seem more intimate than a lover's touch? His cock hardened, and his mouth grew dry as desert sand. Reaching for his coffee, he swallowed the remainder. Finally able to speak, he said, "Thank you, Natalia. This was a delicious meal. And you're a gracious hostess, especially to a stranger."

"We are known for our hospitality to strangers. But strangers need not remain so." She touched her lips with her napkin. "Perhaps you would care for an after-dinner brandy in the drawing room?"

"Yes, that would be excellent." He waited for her to rise, then followed her like the lapdog he was in imminent danger of becoming...if he didn't keep to his assignment.

Natalia vainly tried to quell the eruption of emotions that rumbled through her. She rubbed the fingers of the hand she'd used to touch the stranger; they still prickled as if she'd slept on them and sensation was just now returning.

This man—this Jared Fields—was a mystery. Polished and polite. Clean. Intelligent. What game was he playing? As much as she desired to bed him straightaway, she wouldn't. Not with so much still unknown.

Only a step behind her, his manly presence radiated heat like the afternoon sun. She could feel him. Smell him. *Dios*, she wanted to taste him.

Pausing at the kitchen door, she stopped long enough to tell Sarita to serve them in the sitting room. "The cognac, then go home to Pedro. He'll be missing you. The kitchen can wait until tomorrow." Natalia rubbed her upper arms. "Dress warmly. It's turning colder outside, and storm clouds are gathering."

"*Sí.*" The housekeeper nodded, tucking her head in an attempt to hide her knowing smile. Of all the people in the world, Sarita knew what Natalia had had to put up with. The abuse. The absence of anything resembling a kind word. Indeed, Sarita would wish her well with the man in black.

"She doesn't live in?" Jared asked.

"She has sleeping quarters, for when we entertained, but she has a husband and returns most nights after dinner. Now that I'm a widow, my needs are very simple." *Not so simple. Not really.*

"You aren't afraid at night here by yourself?"

"No. The ranch hands normally take turns guarding." She smiled. "*And* when I'm alone, as I am now—well, I'm very adept with the shotgun I keep under my bed."

"Good to know," he said, sounding somewhat amused.

She led the way down the central hall into the sitting room where she'd first met him, then noted the warmth of the room. Or was it the fire within which heated her so? Yet it was turning colder, if the wind whipping up from the arroyo was any indication.

She arranged her skirts carefully and sat. "Please, make yourself comfortable." This time he chose a silk-upholstered wingback chair, leaning back and resting one of his ankles across his knee. Long, lean-muscled legs. He reached for his pocket, then seemed to think better of it and dropped his hand.

"Go ahead. Smoke if you like. I quite savored the aroma of my husband's after-dinner cigar." Little had old Reginald known, when he wasn't around, she and Sarita had enjoyed smoking a cigarillo after a shared dinner in the kitchen.

He smiled as if he'd been caught out. "Thank you. I will." He pulled a cheroot from his inner pocket along with a match. "Nasty habit." He struck the match on the bottom of his boot.

"But so pleasant after a meal, no?"

"Brandy and a cigar—there's nothing better...almost." His steely gaze warmed as he watched for her response over his cigar.

"And what do you consider better than an after-dinner brandy and cigar?"

"Well..." Jared cleared his throat, his tan cheeks darkening. "There *are* other pleasures... Those not suited to the drawing room."

His slow drawl of the last phrase left no doubt in her mind of his meaning. An unwilling bark of laughter forced itself from her throat. "I fear my late husband would have disagreed with you."

He shot her a rueful smile, lifting one side of his mustache. "*His* misfortune."

"He'll never know." No, Reginald had spent his time whoring and drinking at the Silver Queen. *Bastardo.* Someone had done her a tremendous favor in killing him. *Muchas gracias.* She hoped they never caught the man.

A gust of wind blew through the sitting room, causing the candles to flare and flicker. Two guttered out. "Sarita must have not latched the door securely." She rose from the settee. "I'll double-check it."

Natalia rushed to the front door, found it shut and secured. The iron handle was icy cold to her touch. Shaking her head, she warily opened the door and was stunned by the sight of snow at least three to four inches deep as far as she could see. Even more amazing was the wind blowing snow until she couldn't make out any familiar landmarks.

Surely it wasn't this bad when Sarita left. True, there had been the threat of storm clouds in the afternoon, but it was early in the year to expect such a storm. Although her housekeeper was no longer in sight, she called her name. Her efforts were wasted, lost in the howl of the wind. She should have remained here. Her home wasn't far, but in a blizzard like this, how would she find it?

Chapter Four

Jared sipped the cognac, relishing the rich taste. One thing for sure, Montrose had kept a fine cellar. Natalia returned with a swish of silk, her dark eyes wide with alarm. Setting the brandy snifter on the side table, he straightened and leaned forward. "What is it?"

"It's snowing—three to four inches already—a blizzard. Sarita will never make it home. Why would she have left in a storm like this? I tried calling after her, but she was already out of sight, and the wind..." Natalia's distress over her servant was obvious as she covered her mouth and nose with her hands, shaking her head. "I have to find her. Bring her back."

Jared rose. "Let me see." He strode to the door and whipped it open. All he could see was a raging white wall of gusting wind and snow. Impossible to see beyond the porch, much less any farther. Whether Natalia's servant would make it home was doubtful. At least the woman knew the area. He, for one, would never risk heading out in this mess. Returning to town wasn't an option. Not tonight. Not on an unfamiliar road. Shoving the door closed against the onslaught of wind, he turned back to find Natalia had followed. "You can't go out there."

"You don't understand. I *have* to. Sarita raised me after my mother died." She rushed for the door.

He stopped her by pulling her into his arms, more to comfort than control her. "She knows the way home. Her horse will get her there. You said it's not far."

"I can't just stand here and do nothing!"

"No, you can't. We don't know how long this weather is going to last. We have to make preparations." He'd experienced snowstorms back East, but they were nothing compared to what he'd experienced in Kansas. One winter, a blizzard had come on suddenly with such fierce intensity that animals had died where they stood. "Where's the firewood? What about your animals? We have to make sure they're taken care of."

She started shaking in his arms. Her gaze met his, but her chin trembled as she told him, "There's a stack of firewood behind the stable—don't know how much. It doesn't usually snow this early. We've had a mild fall."

"Focus, Natalia." He set his hands on her shoulders and gave her a little shake. "We don't have much time."

"T-the cattle and drivers are already in La Mesa at the railroad, waiting for transport. My horse is in the stables. Yours too. We keep a cow for milking. Some hens in the henhouse behind the barn."

"Anyone else here? The ranch hand who took my horse?"

"No, he would've taken care of the horses before he left for town."

"Food? We're going to need food."

"The wine cellar—Reginald converted what used to be

the root cellar into storage for wine, but there's plenty of food laid in." Her brows drew together as she gazed into his eyes. "How long do you think this is going to last anyway?"

"A day. A week. Can't tell. This one is starting off bad. I've seen at least one that went on for two weeks."

Shooting him a sharp glance, she stepped back. "Have an abundance of blizzards in St. Louis, do they?"

"It was a hunting trip," he said smoothly, and not a lie, although he'd been hunting a man rather than game. "My party was caught for several days. Long enough that some of the men were looking like they might be pretty tasty."

Her gasp told him she believed his half-truth. "You wouldn't have."

He shrugged. "It's happened before."

A mixture of disbelief and realization in her eyes, she nodded slowly. "Yes, the Donner expedition was a long time before I was born, but I read about it." She sagged against the wall. "You think it could be that bad?"

"I won't lie. It could get very bad before it's over."

Natalia ran her hands back through her hair, loosening several strands, softening her appearance, making her seem more vulnerable. A vulnerability which was more than appealing, but which he had no time to take advantage of. Every second counted if they were going to survive.

"Grain for the horses?"

"In the stable, but how are we...?"

"Not we—*I'll* see to them before it gets any worse. Is there any rope in the house?"

Her beautiful face twisted into a frown. "I don't know of any, but I'm sure there's plenty in the stables."

"So I just have to make it to the stables and run a guideline back to the house."

"You don't know your way. You'll get lost." She worried her bottom lip with her teeth. "I know. I can tear bed linens into strips first and tie them together. Then you can use that as a guide to get back to the house." She nodded. "My husband's clothes are still here. You'll need a heavy coat and scarf, and some heavier trousers"

He grinned. "Works for me."

Natalia ran down the hall to her husband's bedchamber. Another bone of contention early in their marriage had been his refusal to sleep with her in her bedchamber. Given his increasing demands and penchant for rough treatment, she was grateful he didn't. Having a room of her own was her only refuge.

She threw open the door to the chifforobe and pulled out the heaviest coat. Normally, it would've been packed away, but Sarita had aired his winter garments right before he was killed.

Her heart clenched at the thought of Sarita being lost in the blizzard. Such a good woman. She deserved better than freezing to death. Natalia fought back the tears, even as she continued to rummage for one of Reginald's old scarves.

Upon finding one, she headed to the linen press. As much as she hated destroying the linens her late husband had insisted on ordering from one of the finest stores in New York, surviving this blizzard far outweighed the need for luxurious bed coverings.

"Natalia."

She glanced up at Jared, her heart filling with gratitude she didn't have to weather the storm alone. "Follow me," she said, leading him into her own bedchamber, where it was warmer. "You'll to have to help me with this." She passed him a stack of sheets. "The stables are quite a distance from the back of the hacienda."

His gaze widened, then narrowed. "Are you talking a few hundred yards or miles?"

"Not miles," she said with a smile, shaking her head. "Not even a mile. More like a hundred yards or so."

"Thank God for small favors."

"I'll find shears in Sarita's sleeping quarters." She set another stack of linens on her bed, then rushed from the room. Her *bedroom*, a fact very much on her mind.

Jared watched her retreating form. "Two pair, I hope?" he called. Tearing the linens and knotting them into a makeshift tether could take all night. He'd made it as far as her bedroom, and yet all thoughts—*almost* all thoughts—of seducing her were of secondary import.

Before he could consider their situation any further, he heard her rapid footsteps on the tile floor. Triumph flushed her cheeks as she held two pair of shears aloft.

He took one pair. "Did no one ever think to tell you shouldn't run with a pair of shears, much less two?"

"*Sí.*" She pulled an expression so innocent she could've passed for a nun. "Don't be such an old woman," she said with a laugh.

"Glad that you can laugh, given our situation." Hopefully there wouldn't be tears before it ended.

Throughout the next couple of hours, they cut then tore the bed linens into strips, both of them sitting on the floor with heaps of strips piled around them as they knotted the ends together. Try as he might to keep his mind on surviving the storm, it was damned difficult. Her lively energy as she knotted and chatted about trivial matters was hypnotic and pulled at his being. When he'd first met her, she'd seemed very conscious of her appearance and allure. Now she seemed oblivious to everything except the task at hand...and damned if he didn't find her even more desirable.

Jared shivered. The room was colder. Or did it seem so from not being able to touch her? He stood to stretch his legs. "The fire in here is almost out." He glanced over his shoulder. "I'll check the fireplace in the drawing room as well." He scooped up a section of the knotted sheeting. "Can't wait any longer. This has to be enough. I need to bring in more wood before we freeze."

"Might it not be over by morning?" She gazed up at him, her eyes wide and dark as pools of water in moonlight.

The hope in her voice gutted him. He rubbed his eyes and shook his head. "If I were a gambling man, I wouldn't bet on it."

"What if these aren't long enough? What will you do then? Come back? I'll keep knotting until..." She sighed, signaling her hope had turned into desperation.

"If I can see the stables, I'll go on."

Before pulling on Montrose's heavy coat, he stirred the fire, adding the last logs of mesquite to the fireplaces in her bedchamber and the sitting room. "Now, which door is closest to the stables?"

"The kitchen. I'll show you." Holding a pile of knotted linens, she led him down the hall and back through the dining room, then through another doorway into a large, tiled kitchen. Homey and warm. Understandable why Natalia preferred sharing a simple dinner with her housekeeper to eating alone in the pretentious dining room. He couldn't help but remember the hours he'd spent as a boy at home, waiting while the cook baked cookies for him and his brother.

"There's a courtyard and a gate. Beyond the gate, the stable's a hundred yards, straight ahead."

He nodded, then tried to open the door. Putting his shoulder to it, he shoved and forced the door open. The wind howled like a banshee, driving stinging cold snow into the kitchen. The heavy, soggy snow had drifted higher than expected. Over a foot.

Natalia handed him one end of a linen strip. "Tie this around your wrist...just in case I have to come find you."

The thought of her trying to find him in the midst of this blizzard shook him. He set his hands on her shoulders and gazed into her black-as-night eyes. "Promise me you won't come out in this."

"No! If you don't return when I think you should, I *will* come after you."

"There's no way to estimate how long it'll take for me to see to the animals and bring in more firewood. Promise you'll stay inside. If something happens to me, then you still have a chance of surviving. You have food. You may get cold, but these walls are a foot thick. You'll be all right...*as long as you stay put.*"

She folded her arms across her chest, her beautiful

mouth drawing into a pout. "If you say so."

Her attitude said differently, but damn it, he hated to go out into the storm without tasting her lips just once.

Still, kissing her would be extremely forward. Hesitating for a second, he pulled her closer and planted a light kiss on those delectable lips. Granted, it was more of a peck that a true kiss. He wanted her as desperately as a soldier going off to war. So what if it was war with the elements?

To his surprise, her arms encircled his neck. She pressed her lush breasts against his chest and kissed him back full on the mouth. Passionately. God, she smelled better than any woman had a right to. And her lips were as demanding as his should've been. Yet soft and yielding as...fresh, homemade butter. If he could eat her now, he would.

Damn.

The hunger of her response shook him, or was the hunger all his? A passionate woman, bursting with life, intelligence—more than capable of reaching out for what she wanted and grabbing it with both hands. But was she capable of having her husband murdered?

He'd have to know. Soon. But not now.

Summoning all his willpower, he ended the kiss. Took a step back. "Time to go."

Natalia tried to cling to him. "No!"

"Have to." He nodded, swallowing the knot in his throat. What man wouldn't rather stay in Natalia's arms than venture out into the worst blizzard he'd ever seen?

"Men!" She stamped her foot. "You and your *machismo*. You're all alike. Go on and brave the blizzard. Don't expect me to come looking for your cold, frozen body. *Sí*, I'll just

stay here where, for the moment, it's reasonably warm."
She turned her back to him. "If I'm not found until the
spring thaw, who is there to care? Not even my mercenary
father. I'm sure he'll be delighted to inherit all my land and
cattle."

Jared wanted to laugh but wisely refrained. A survivor—
that was what the fiery beauty before him was. Natalia
would be all right whether he returned or not.

He pulled on a pair of wool gloves, set his Stetson on his
head, and wrapped the scarf around his neck, covering his
nose and mouth. Without saying another word, he picked
up the makeshift rope and opened the door again. A blast
of searing-cold air hit him, staggering him almost to his
knees. He fastened one end of the tether to his wrist and
the opposite to a section of wrought-iron railing. Then,
sucking in a breath, he headed out into the wall of white.

Natalia pulled the shawl tighter around her shoulders
and watched Jared disappear into the storm. Involuntarily,
her hand went to her mouth. She could almost feel his lips
on hers. She'd felt his desire too, pressing hard into her
belly. He wanted her. Why couldn't he have stayed just a
little longer? They could have kept each other warm
through the night. Morning would have been soon enough
for him to play the hero.

Madre de Dios, please let him be all right. Still, she
couldn't just stand there at the door waiting for his return.
Coffee—she would keep it brewing as long as the wood
lasted. He would be nearly frozen through when he came
back. And he *would* come back to her. He would. He must.

She spent the next few minutes relighting the cookstove, then set the coffeepot on the hot plate. Walking over to the window, she held her breath. She wiped away a rime of frost from the glass in an attempt to see the makeshift line or any sign of his progress. But all she could see through the window was snow blowing sideways. Beyond that...nothing.

A tremor shook her body, causing her to rub her upper arms. Someone walking over her grave? Perhaps this hacienda would prove to be the death of her. It certainly hadn't brought Reginald any luck. But then, he'd thought money was more important than luck. When he'd first approached her father about purchasing the hacienda and all the land with it, he hadn't counted on her father's insistence that Reginald should marry his daughter as part of the devil's own bargain. After the financial transaction, her father moved to San Francisco, married a rich widow and bought a fine hotel. And Natalia was left to suffer the living death of a loveless, passionless marriage.

The rattle and bubble of the coffeepot as it started percolating drew her attention back to the cookstove. She smiled. The sound brought back happy memories of the busy mornings before her mother had died. How different Natalia's life might've been if her mother had lived instead of dying along with the baby boy who would've been her brother.

A wave of sadness enveloped her...that and worry.

Sarita, who'd cared for Natalia since her mother's death, was likely lost in the storm. Natalia crossed herself, saying a quiet prayer for Sarita and Jared both.

Chapter Five

Never seen such a storm. Not like this.

One step at a time, Jared trudged through snow that drifted higher and higher, by the second, it seemed. Unable to see more than a foot in front of his face, was he heading anywhere near the stables? *Straight ahead*, she'd said.

Sure thing, if his lids weren't trying to freeze shut. He swiped at the ice clinging to his lashes and sucked in a lungful of blistering-cold air. The wool scarf over his mouth and nose helped some, but it couldn't overcome the wind and the nut-freezing cold. He tugged on the strip of sheeting. Still plenty of slack in this lifeline of his.

What he wouldn't give for a pair of snowshoes.

More interminable steps. A hundred yards was nothing unless one was in a blizzard to end all blizzards. Damned impossible to tell how far he'd come or how much farther he had to go.

Without warning, he stepped into a hole. His arms flailed as he attempted to maintain his balance, but there was nothing to grab or hold on to. Crashing down, he tumbled into a waist-high drift. Snow covered his head, swathed his face with its icy wetness. Using one end of the scarf, he wiped it away, then rolled over to his knees before rising to stand.

He tugged his wrist. He'd lost the strip of cloth tethering him to the ranch house.

Damnation.

Frustration cut through his gut as he removed his gloves, stuffed them in his pockets, and then ran his hands through the piles of snow. Couldn't keep that up forever. Frostbite. Worse, the fall had disoriented him. Unable to tell which direction he originally was headed, he circled slowly. Behind him, the snow fell so hard it obliterated his trail from the house. *First, find the damned line.* Without it, he'd never find his way back.

Down on his knees, he began a systematic search. Ignoring the biting chill, he kept searching for the tether until his fingers grew numb and clumsy, feeling like thick sausages. Wouldn't work. Couldn't keep this up. He stopped, removed the gloves from his pockets, and slipped his freezing fingers into the lined leather gloves. While not exactly warm, the gloves were a hell of a lot better than nothing.

Back on his feet, he attempted once more to get his bearings. Had to move forward, back...whatever. Staying in one spot wasn't an option. When he'd left Natalia, the snow was blowing from the northeast. That meant he could keep moving *straight ahead* by keeping the blowing snow to his right...as long as the wind hadn't changed direction without his noticing.

He waded through the deepening drifts, fighting the urge to say to hell with it. But death lay with that decision. Step by never-ending step, he continued what he'd already decided was a fool's journey.

He had no warning. One second there was nothing but snow; the next, he ran smack into the stables. At least he hoped it was the stables. It had taken them so long to make the guideline, the snow was waist-high. Now to find the entrance and clear away enough to get inside.

IIe found the stable doors without any problem. Fortunately, the wind and snow were coming from the opposite direction, resulting in a huge drift at the rear of the stable. After knocking away the ice and snow, he raised the bar on the stable door, then pried the door open, just enough to squeeze through. He heard a nervous whinny from one of the horses. "Easy," he said to calm the animal.

Out of the blowing wind. Finally. He leaned against the wall to catch his breath, then stomped his boots and brushed the snow from Montrose's coat. Removing his Stetson, he slapped it against his thigh, then set it back on his head.

Okay. The smell of horse, manure, and feed grain wafted upward. His nose wrinkled, but it was the normal smell of a stable. He waited until his eyes adjusted to the dark. Using the bit of light filtering through the door, he surveyed the interior of the stable. Two horses, Midnight and Natalia's mare, possibly a dapple gray. Difficult to tell without a source of light.

Stopping long enough to soothe each animal, he hoped they would tolerate the length of confinement a blizzard required. He walked deeper into the stable and found the cow the ranch kept. A cow that would require *milking* in the morning. Never one of his skills. Had the fiery Natalia ever ventured to milk one?

He quickly located grain for the horses and feed for the cow and chickens. Water would be more of a necessity for the animals. Could he melt enough to keep them alive for who knew how long?

No point in messing around. They wouldn't require feeding until the morning. Best locate the rope and find his way back to the house...and Natalia Montrose.

Whether she was an innocent and apparently neglected wife or a cold-hearted bitch who ordered the death of her husband didn't really matter at this stage.

Survival did.

Outside, the wind continued its incessant howl. Pacing the length of the kitchen, Natalia covered her ears. Would it never stop?

How long had Jared been gone? It seemed like hours and hours had passed, but when she walked into the central hall and glanced at the long case clock, it showed eleven o'clock. He'd been gone a mere hour. Pulling her shawl tighter around her shoulders, she shivered. The embers still glowed in the fireplace and put off a small degree of heat.

At least *she* was warm enough. Jared was out in the freezing cold, a man of action charging to the rescue—not a financial counselor. Maybe she *was* safe while he was taking all the risks, but she didn't want to think about spending days or weeks alone and stranded by the storm. If something happened to him...

She clenched her fists and rushed to her bedchamber. Throwing open the doors to the chifforobe, she pulled out the denim trousers she hadn't worn since she'd married, along with a heavy flannel shirt. No, Reginald wouldn't hear of her riding about their land in breeches. It was full riding habit or she could just stay inside and embroider.

Quickly, she pulled off her skirt and shirtwaist. Fortunately, this one had buttons in the front. Sarita wasn't needed to unbutton it. No, her dear friend was probably lying in the snow somewhere, dying or dead. Natalia's throat closed with the thought of losing her only friend. Why hadn't she asked her to spend the night instead of sending her home?

The answer was obvious. No doubt, Sarita noticed the heated interest arcing between Natalia and the *muy* handsome Jared and left them alone on purpose, never suspecting her decision might prove fatal. And maybe she just wanted to get home to spend a warm evening in her husband's arms.

Once Natalia had dressed for the extreme weather, she strode to the kitchen. *You can do this. You have to do this. Jared should be back by now.* Using her shoulder, much as Jared had, she planted her feet and set her back into shoving open the door. With a loud groan, the door opened enough for her to slip though.

Madre de Dios. The snow was now to her mid-thighs, and drifts were higher than her waist. Well, it wasn't going to get any easier. She used her hands to scoop a path in the snow in front of her, attempting to find where Jared tied one end of the sheet rope. The wind was blowing from the northeast, and icy pellets pelted her face like stinging nettles. There was no turning back now. Jared was out there somewhere, and he'd definitely been gone too long.

When she made it to the wrought-iron porch support where he'd tied one end of the guide line, she saw it was covered by at least a foot of snow. By now he should've tied his end to something in the stable. Yet it wasn't as taut as she'd expected. Was he truly lost?

If she followed its knotted length, what would she find? The living, breathing man who stirred her beyond anything she'd ever imagined or a frozen lump who'd given his life to care for their horses?

Of course, he had to be the hero. More like a futile Don Quixote. Madness to continue any farther. But just as he had risked his life for her, in good conscience, she couldn't just return to the ranch house and consign him to whatever fate had in store. Grasping the knotted sheet as her guide, she waded deeper into the snow.

The unrelenting wind knocked her backward more than once. *Madre de Dios*, she was as strong as any woman she knew. And stronger than many men, if determination and sheer grit counted for anything. This wind and snow and ice—she wouldn't let them defeat her.

Not after all she'd been through. Not now. Not ever.

Exhausted by what seemed like hours of slogging through the heavy, packed snow, Natalia was more than ready to concede the folly of her actions. The knotted rope was slack, no longer attached to Jared. No longer attached to anything. Had she walked over his body buried in one of the drifts which were already shoulder-deep some places?

If so, she'd never find him. Someone still had to check on the animals in the stable. She would have to do as Jared had intended and bring back the rope, which would act as a guide between the ranch house and the stable. She wouldn't allow her mare to freeze or starve to death, or any of the other animals. The hacienda was her responsibility now, and she would care for it alone, as long as necessary.

She rubbed the frozen tears from her lashes, sniffed, and immediately regretted inhaling a blast of air that burned inside her chest. Jared was such a virile man. To think of his death saddened her, no matter how short their acquaintance. Whatever his true reasons for seeking her out, they wouldn't have kept him from her bed. She knew when a man wanted her, just as she'd known when her husband hadn't.

Dios, it hurt to breathe. So tired. Every step a herculean trial.

She stumbled, falling to her knees. Her eyelids so heavy. Just needed a moment to rest. The snow so soft like a down mattress. And warm...like a blanket.

Chapter Six

The wind continued to howl, increasing in intensity from earlier. Tying one end of rope to a sturdy post, Jared secured it with two square knots. No way would it come undone. He *could* spend the rest of the night in the barn, which would save another trip in the morning. Nah. He shook his head and hefted the bale of rope onto his shoulder. One way or another, he had to go back. Didn't matter that he'd warned Natalia to stay inside; he didn't trust her as far as he could sling her over his shoulder and toss her across the Rio Grande.

Fiery. Passionate. And stubborn as all get-out. Might take it into that pretty head of hers to see what was taking him so long. Last thing he needed was the subject of his inquiry getting lost in a blizzard, leaving too many unanswered questions regarding her husband's death.

No point in waiting. Storm wasn't going to let up. The door wouldn't open wide enough for his shoulders and the rope. He shoved the rope out the door, then squeezed through and picked up the rope once again. For a moment, he stood still, searching for his bearings. The wind still blew from the northeast.

Keep the wind to the left on the trip back. Still dark. No moon visible. The going was tougher than the trip out. No fucking wonder. Snow was a foot deeper too. Most of his path had filled in while he was in the stable.

Just keep the wind to your left.

He hadn't gone far when he stumbled and fell over an obstruction in the snow. Digging frantically, he uncovered a body. He swept off the Stetson covering the face and discovered long black hair spilling over the snow. "Son of a bitch!"

Her face was waxen. Her pale lids gave not so much as a flutter. He shook her. "Natalia!" And still no response. He pulled her flaccid body from the drift, intending to take her back to the stables. The house was too far to carry her *and* a large bale of rope. He needed to warm her up, and quick, if she was to survive the freezing cold.

He should've known she'd pull something like this. He trudged forward, thankful the stable wasn't far and he could still make out his trail. His breathing grew ragged. As small as she was, her body was dead weight, and the cold had made him sluggish.

Hell! Both of them were in danger of freezing to death if he didn't get a move on.

Ahead of him, the hulking darkness grew. The stable.

He would have to set her down to open the door open again. He sucked in another breath and laid her down with a soft thump. Strength fading fast, he pulled the door open and took her by the booted ankles and dragged her inside, away from the cold, then collapsed on his butt, completely exhausted.

By comparison, the stables felt heated, but they

wouldn't for long if he didn't close the door. A minute more and he'd get up. He *would*.

All right, maybe it took more than a couple breaths before his foggy brain cleared. Damnation! He got to his feet, pulled the rope inside, then dragged on the door until it closed. Natalia still hadn't moved. He knelt over her and put his head to her chest. Yes, he could still hear a heartbeat.

"Natalia. You're safe. We're in the stables." No good. He pulled her back to an empty stall, where straw covered the floor. An old horse blanket was folded over the stall divider. That would work, but she sure as hell wasn't going to like what he was about to do next. Unfortunately, in her extreme condition, he couldn't think of any other way to warm her up.

He grabbed the wool blanket and knelt beside her. He threw aside his borrowed coat and unbuttoned his shirt, shivering as the air hit his bare skin. Then he pulled her arms from the wet coat she wore and unbuttoned her flannel shirt. Unable to see in the low light, he couldn't resist touching her. The silken smooth skin was icy cold and a faint pulse beat in her throat.

She'd probably kill him when she woke up. *If* she woke up.

Smothering. Warm and yet cold. Shaking. Natalia struggled, then, aware of bare skin next to hers, she relaxed. A dream. One of *those* dreams that left her shaken and wanting more than a mere dream-lover could give. She let out a contented sigh. Might as well enjoy the dream while it lasted. So much better than the snow outside.

The snow outside?

Shivering, she tried to inch up on her elbows...and couldn't. Something warm and heavy lay on top of her. Panicked and unable to see anything in the inky blackness, she began to struggle.

"Talia, it's all right."

At the sound of Jared's voice, her eyes flew open. "What are you doing on top of me? Where *are* we?"

"We're in the stable. I found you outside in the snow. You were almost frozen."

"So you brought me back into the stables and just thought you'd take my clothes off? And yours too, while you were at it? Was that your reward for saving my life?" She twisted and turned, trying to get out from under him. "Move!"

"You were almost frozen to death. I had to warm you up." She felt his fingers brush the hair from her cheek in a soothing gesture.

"So stripping me naked was the way to do it?" She pushed at his unyielding bare chest. "Get off me."

"Body-to-body heat. That's what you needed."

"No, I beg to differ. That's what *you* needed." Ever since she'd first seen him in her sitting room, she'd thought about taking him to her bed and riding him until they were both exhausted, but it should've been with her permission. *Dios*, she'd missed everything. Maybe not everything after all, since she suddenly became aware of his hard cock jabbing her belly. "Just what happened here?"

"Nothing happened, except I saved your ungrateful life."

"But your—um, body is very aroused."

"You're a beautiful woman, Natalia." His voice had a low, sensual quality that thrilled her. "Any man would be aroused."

"You *looked* at my body? *Sí*, I'm sure *that* was a vital part of saving my life."

"I *am* a man."

"That is very obvious." And she was a woman, and *Dios*, this man's cock was so close to where she desperately needed it.

"In case you haven't noticed, it's damned dark in here. Couldn't see much. More by feel."

"And I'm sure you felt plenty." She squirmed against his hard cock. "But you know, I think this body-heat thing is working," she admitted.

Over her, he shrugged. "You're alive. I'd say it's working." He caressed her breast, tweaking the nipple.

"Yes," she gasped, as a thrill of pleasure shot to her core. Of their own volition, her arms went around his back. "Are you sure you needed to get so naked?"

"If something works, don't question it."

He leaned forward and kissed her neck, then nibbled on the lobe of her ear. A guttural moan erupted from her throat. Her thighs parted. "Now."

"No."

She went up on one elbow. Was the man crazy? Or was he another man who couldn't bear to make love to her. "No? You have me naked as the day I was born. What do you mean 'no'?"

"Too soon. There's more."

His voice, low and seductive with the hint of promise, sent a shiver up her spine. More? She liked the sound of that. "I *want* more."

"Be nice, Talia. I'll give you what you want...and more. On my terms. Not yours."

He slipped his hand between their bodies and slid a calloused finger in and out of her pussy, then flicked her clit with his thumb. Her inner muscles contracted from his intimate touch. Her hips rose to meet him, but he pulled away. Whimpers of need emanated from her throat. "Don't leave me like this."

He chuckled, a deep rumble she could feel through his chest. "Not going anywhere. It's still snowing and it's cold outside. Don't be so impatient."

Natalia let out a sigh of frustration. Jared didn't understand. No, he couldn't. Reginald had never loved her. Never wanted her. Even taunted her, saying she was nothing more than a whore for wanting his attentions. He seldom took his pleasure with her in the normal fashion, and never, ever considered her need for release.

"It's going to be a long night. And I have no intention of leaving you high and dry."

Although he couldn't see it, she smiled up at him. He *did* understand.

He dipped his head and kissed her, softly at first, then harder. His tongue parted her lips and brushed against hers. Hunger drove her as she thrust her tongue to meet his. His calloused hands were on her breasts. She gasped for air as he pulled her nipples, teasing them into tight pebbles. He licked and sucked one, nipping it with his teeth. Exquisite sensations of pleasure shot to her lower belly and then to her core.

She caressed the sides of his strong face, then splayed

her fingers down to his flat male nipples. He moved his hands to cup her buttocks. Her hips arched, and he nuzzled his face down to her belly, his mustache soft and tickling as he dove farther.

His tongue was wet and warm as he licked between her legs. Her thighs trembled from the unaccustomed onslaught of pleasurable sensations. In the dreams that haunted her unfulfilled nights, she'd never imagined such pleasure.

"You like that, don't you?"

She cared not that he sounded amused. It felt too good to lie. "*Sí.* Very much." She wriggled her hips, anticipating what came next.

Again he chuckled. Who knew making love was a matter of amusement? Not she. Not until now.

"Lift your legs...high," he demanded.

Somewhat glad of the dark, she fought against the heavy blanket covering both of them, spread and drew up her legs. She was totally vulnerable to whatever he wanted. He knelt between her thighs and buried his face between them. His tongue danced around her clit, alternately sucking and licking it faster and faster.

Her legs jittered as waves of pleasure crashed through her body, stunning her with their intensity, her inner muscles clenching and releasing. "*Dios,*" she moaned.

Jared quickly covered her mouth with his hand. "Careful, you'll scare the horses."

Lying beside her before she regained consciousness, he'd been terrified he hadn't found her soon enough. That she still might die. Now, if he didn't have her soon, his cock felt like it would explode. He slid his hand between them, grabbed his dick and rubbed the head up and down her wet cleft, then thrust home. Driving into the depths of her slick warmth, he propped on his elbows and cradled her face in his hands, kissing her arched neck. Her slender legs tightened around his waist as she rose to meet each thrust.

His hunger matched hers. The more he thrust, the more he wanted her. Needed her. Her pussy tightened around his cock, squeezing and releasing him until he was on the verge of losing all control. Beneath him, her writhing body seemed to burn with the fire of their passion. With his last bit of control, he slowed the pace of his thrusts, focusing on the tight, silken feel of her wet pussy.

"Faster, please." Her plea was drawn out, slow and low, her breathing ragged in his ear as her heated body bucked with each responding thrust.

In spite of his intention to pull out before it was too late, he surrendered. With a groan gathering from the very depths of his balls, he pumped into her heated core until he exploded like a charge of dynamite. Talia's nails dug into his shoulders as she climaxed with him.

Gathering her in his arms, he rolled to his side, taking her with him. He gently brushed back the hair spilling across her face. Like his, her face and chest were damp with perspiration from their lovemaking.

"Thank you," she said with gasping, warm breaths that tickled his ear.

He tilted his head to the side. "For the fuck or for saving your life?"

"Both." He felt her shoulders lift in a shrug. "However, if you hadn't saved my life, I suppose there would have been no...fucking."

"You suppose right, Talia." He shifted until her body was spooned in his arms, her firm ass tucked close into his crotch. "Still have to keep your body warm." Although it was damned warm under the layers of their coats and the horse blanket.

A sigh of contentment was the only reply she made, her body relaxing sweetly along with his. "Talia?"

This time all he heard was a soft snore.

Damnation, it would be a long night before he could relax enough to sleep. The wind picked up, howling like a hungry wolf on the trail of prey. A shiver ran through his body. They'd have to dig themselves out in the morning to get back to the ranch house, but for now, they were alive and out of the worst of the blizzard.

Talia's head rested on his arm. At least *she* could sleep. The storm wasn't what was keeping him awake. He was here for a reason, not to fuck a confession out of Montrose's widow. Once the blizzard was over, he planned to stay close and observe her actions. He didn't want to believe Montrose's father was right in his suspicions. Natalia Montrose was temperamental and proud, but if she had killed her husband, she'd have done it herself in a fit of anger.

She would have carved Reginald's heart out and fed it to coyotes—yes, he could see her doing something like that. But pay someone else to kill him? Not her style.

Chapter Seven

White everywhere. Drowning in an icy sea, enveloped by the cold, she fought her way to the surface. Chills ran through her. Swim. Swim. She willed her arms and legs to move. Too cold. Too tired. Too afraid to die. A scream erupted from her throat. Her arms flailed...

"Talia. Talia. Wake up. It's a nightmare. You're safe."

Confused, she opened her eyes. Dark. "Did the candles go out?"

"We're in the barn. Remember?" His tone held a note of disbelief.

It all came rushing back. Falling in the snow and awakening in his arms, her bare breasts skin-to-skin with his furry chest. "*Sí*, I remember," she said with a grin, even if he couldn't see her expression. How could she forget the first time she'd achieved satisfaction that wasn't the result of her own fevered manipulations?

"You warmed my body with yours"—she squirmed to face him, her hands playing up and down the strong muscles of his back—"and then you proceeded to take full advantage of my vulnerability. I thought maybe you were a gentleman, but alas, I fear you are the rankest of opportunists."

The feel of his cock growing hard against her belly drew her mouth into a smile. So, he enjoyed her touching him. Good. She reveled in an unaccustomed power. Maybe that was why Reginald would never respond to her—he couldn't risk giving her the smallest amount of control over him.

"What's wrong?" Jared asked, caressing her cheek. "A minute ago, you were all soft and warm. Now your body's tense."

Natalia shook her head. "Just remembering how it was before. I was always...*tense.*"

"He didn't know how to please you?" Jared's lips were at the hollow of her neck, and he traced a path of fire down her skin with a single finger, sending rivulets of desire to pool in her lower belly.

"He never tried." She wanted to beg for more of his touch. Would have been happy to get on her knees if necessary. Her hips seemed to lift of their own accord as his fingers slipped into the valley between her thighs.

"Last time, I was pretty quick on the trigger. It's been a while for me."

"And *this* time?" She couldn't help but tease him by asking, "Am I still in danger of freezing to death, *Señor* Fields?"

"You're in no danger. This time it's because you want it. Do you...Talia?"

She loved the way he shortened her name and the sexy tone he used when he said it. "*Sí.* And whether you know it or not, you are still saving my life." Possibly her sanity as well. *Dios*, what a drab, passionless life she'd lived for eight miserable years. Whether Jared was a financial adviser, as he said, or the worst type of drifter and confidence man, he'd saved her life and given her the kind of pleasure of which she'd only dreamed.

And once the blizzard was over, she would learn more about what he was up to, but for now...she needed another fucking.

She clamped her thighs around his hand and began to writhe, moving her hips up and down. "I want more...now."

"Happy to oblige you, ma'am."

Smiling in the dark, she opened her thighs and reached for his hard cock to guide him home. She locked her ankles around his waist, and he hugged her to him, then flipped over until he was on his back and she on top, truly able to ride him like the fine stallion of a man he was. She leaned over him, her breasts touching and being tickled by the light fur of his chest. Her nipples tightened into thrilling beads of sensation.

He snared one of her breasts, clamped on to one of her *tetillas* and grazed it lightly with his teeth, sending spikes of pleasure to her pussy. His hands cupping her ass, he thrust deeply as she rocked up and down on his cock, slowly at first, then, as the heat began to build, she increased the pace until her inner muscles tightened hard on his cock and wouldn't let go. *Dios*, she'd never felt anything like this before.

Her body on fire, she rode until something deep within her shattered and sent her flying over the edge. He increased the rhythm of his thrusts, each one deeper than the one before until he seemed a part of her. She arched her back against his raised knees and emitted a low, shuddering moan which crescendoed into a scream... Or would have if he hadn't clamped his hand over her mouth. He continued pumping into her until, a few seconds later, he gave a final thrust and groaned.

Her body slick with perspiration, she giggled and fell across his chest, burrowing her face into his neck. "Now who's going to upset the horses?"

Nuzzling her ear, he gasped for breath. "Maybe they'll get used to hearing your strange, catlike noises."

"Maybe they will." If she had anything to say about it, they would. Her body was warm and relaxed against his firm one, as if hot water flowed through her veins. How would she ever allow this man to leave her sight and go back to his supposed dreary life of watching over other people's money? Making him her prisoner of love would make her much happier. Even the thought pulled her lips into a smile.

His mouth found hers. "You're smiling," he whispered, never moving his lips from hers.

"And you're not?" she said, challenging him. Tenderly, she brushed back the shock of hair from his forehead.

"Oh, most definitely I am, Talia. Can't remember smiling this much—not in a long time."

"Then stop talking and smiling and *kiss* me." She snaked her arms around his neck, rubbing her cheek against his prickly one.

Taking her in his arms, he rolled to his side, pulling her with him, kissing her, punishing her already swollen lips, his tongue finding hers, battling for dominance. A small sigh escaped her lips as she snuggled into his warm embrace. Never had she felt so complete. So womanly. So— dare she think it—loved.

*

The next morning dawned with a cold so cold Natalia thought her tender nipples would surely freeze and fall off from frostbite before she could pull on her clothing. And if *she* was worried, there was another person's important body part that she'd hate... *How absurd.* They weren't going to lose their valuable body parts, not if she could help it. She let out a low bark of laughter.

Daylight brought a stream of light into the stable. Jared, who was also getting dressed, glanced at her. "What's so damned amusing?"

"I was thinking you'd better hurry before something very important to both of us gets frostbitten."

His forehead furrowed, pulling his thick, dark brows together. "You think it'd be funny if my cock froze?"

"Well, it is rather exposed at the moment." His dick rose like a limestone pillar. "Could happen if you're not careful."

"Don't you worry, Natalia. I learned a long time ago how to care for my prick. It's instinctive among the male gender."

"No doubt. Indeed, Reginald deemed his cock so precious, I was forced to worship at its altar more times than I could count. Sadly, he never returned the favor."

"That is—was—his loss. Can't understand it myself."

He moved closer and caressed her cheek, filling her heart with a rush of new-found emotions. "I'm glad to know there isn't anything wrong with me, after all."

"*You* are a gift to mankind, and I'm honored you shared yourself with me." He swept a theatrically low bow.

She held back a giggle. The man was still naked from the

waist down. And while she still could, she took in the sight of his long, strong-muscled thighs. Lean hipped and flat bellied, he had a slightly furry chest with a whorl of black that dipped to a patch of black hair where his thick cock jutted at her in a most friendly manner.

"What?"

"Observing my lover," she said. "It was so dark last night..."

"Yes, it was the blind leading the blind." His expression seemed lit from within as he leaned over and placed a quick kiss on her forehead.

"All the same, you did exceptionally well." She smiled, fluttering her lashes for effect, yet feeling abashed at their frank exchange.

He yanked up Reginald's Levi's, cutting off her view. "Someone better mind her own business, or she's going to be the one minus a couple of very pretty..."

He wiggled his eyebrows; then, grinning, he bent to take a nipple in his warm mouth, obliterating all her thoughts of caring for the animals and getting back to the ranch house. Every time he used his mouth on her body, she wanted nothing more than to slide his fine cock between her legs. Her body suffused with heat; she clung to him, wishing they could make love again on the spot.

He shook his head. "Get dressed." His voice was low and raspy. "The horses need to be fed and watered. A cow needs milking."

At that, the sounds of bovine lowing intruded into her fantasy. Pulling up her riding pants, somewhat carefully due to the tenderness between her legs, she nodded. "I know."

They quickly finished dressing. Jared tended to both horses' needs while Natalia milked the cow. "What'll we do with all this milk?" She nodded toward the wooden bucketful of milk with steam rising in the frigid air. "Maybe we could get one bucket back to the house."

"Maybe."

She walked over to her mare's stall and rubbed her nose. "It's going to be all right, Esperanza. It will." Her mare nickered softly under Natalia's touch.

"Trying to convince the mare or yourself?"

"A little of both, I guess."

"Are you ready?" he asked, nodding toward the door.

"To brave the elements? As ready as I'll ever be." Truly, if they never left the stable until the snow melted in the spring, she couldn't imagine a better... Maybe not. She wrinkled her nose as an awareness of the stable smells hit her full force. Horse droppings. Cow patties.

"Good. 'Cause getting back to the ranch house isn't going to be a Sunday stroll." He buttoned the heavy overcoat she'd given him from Reginald's wardrobe. It was a snug fit through the shoulders, but loose through the gut. Reginald had sported quite a belly.

Jared dragged the bale of rope that would be their guideline between the stable and house over to the stable door, then set it down. "First things first. Let's get this door open."

She picked up two shovels, then walked over to the door to stand beside him. "I can help."

Grinning down at her, he took one of the shovels and delivered a slow, deliberate wink. "Wouldn't think of leaving you behind."

Natalia watched as Jared lifted the heavy wooden crossbar securing the stable door. He seemed to put all his weight against the door, but it didn't budge. Setting down her shovel, she said, "Here. Maybe if we both..."

"Can't hurt."

Together they pushed. One inch. Then two. She peeped outside and couldn't believe her eyes. Even though she'd struggled through the storm last night, there was nothing visible but the glare of white snow, glistening almost to her eye level. She swallowed the lump in her throat. Her heart pounded as the reality of their situation hit her. "We're stuck. We can't get out." She tried to keep the panic from sounding in her voice but failed.

"I'll climb up into the loft. We can lower ourselves on the rope. Get out that way. Damn good thing I pulled it in last night after bringing you inside."

She nodded slowly. He sounded so self-assured, so positive his plan would work. Who was this Jared Fields who had a solution for every obstacle? How did a man from the East, a mere financial advisor, become so adept at survival? Who was he really?

If the simple answer was that he was the man who'd saved her life, then questioning his motives served no purpose. His reasons would only count once their ordeal was over. For now, survival was all that mattered.

"There's a ladder over there," she said, pointing toward the back of the stable.

"Right." He gave a quick nod. "Saw it earlier."

He picked up the ladder and propped it on the loft ledge, then grabbed up the bale of rope and began to climb. "What're you waiting for," he said over his shoulder, "an invitation?"

She stuck her tongue out at him and stepped onto the ladder. "You're in my way, *Señor* Fields. Move it."

"The shovels? Bring the shovels, Natalia."

"*Sí, señor. Jefe.*" She jumped from the ladder and grabbed up the two shovels.

"Now see if I'm getting in your way." He climbed slowly but with a grin.

"I shall wait until you are in the loft and will hand you one of the shovels; then I'll come up with the second." She gave him her sweetest smile. Now that they were both encumbered with the weight of the equipment they'd need to dig themselves a trench back to the house, the bucket of milk would have to wait for the next trip. In the cold, it would remain fresh. More likely, it would freeze before they returned later that evening.

Indeed, they would be lucky if they didn't freeze as well. The thought of dying from the cold sent a shiver down her spine. She'd already come so close.

Jared walked to the front of the hayloft and opened the gable door. The wind was still blowing from the northeast, and even though the front of the stable faced the southwest, a tremendous amount of snow had drifted in front of the stable. He shook his head. How the hell would they ever make it back to the house before dark? From his vantage point, he could just make out the faint shadow of the long adobe house. Maybe he ought to leave Talia in the stable where she'd be safe enough for the day or so it would take to clear a trench.

No, with two of them working, it wouldn't take as long. If they didn't make the house before nightfall, they could return to the stable through the cleared portion of the path. Damn him for a fool, but the thought of spending another night in her arms was mighty appealing.

"Hey, *vaquero*! I need some help."

Grinning at her playful tone, he turned and saw Talia peeping over the loft floor. Quickly closing the distance between them, he took the shovel she held and tossed it to the side. "Here you go," he said. He thrust his hand forward, grabbed her wrist and hauled her into the loft.

"*Muchas gracias.*" She smiled up at him, her dark, doe eyes glowing with good humor. Frankly, she made his knees weak and set his heart to hammering faster than it ought. He shook his head. This wasn't the time... "Best get a move on," he said with his gruffest tone. "This is going be the hardest work you've ever done."

The lady snorted in a most unladylike manner. "Like *you've* dug yourself out of a blizzard before?"

He glanced over his shoulder toward the gable door. "I have, but not one like this."

"Hmph. I grew up here. I've seen bad snowstorms before." She strutted confidently over to the loft gable door.

He nodded. "Right." The denim trousers suited her slender body, showing off the very curves he'd grown familiar with the night before, but then he heard a gasp as she peered out the door.

She turned to him, her eyes wide with alarm. "*Dios!* This *is* the worst I've ever seen."

"Yeah." He set to tying one end of the rope bale to an upright support beam. "I'll go down first and clear the snow from the doorway. Otherwise, we won't be able to get back in. Unless you want to shinny up the rope twice a day?" He motioned with a hand-over-hand gesture.

"No, but that doesn't mean I couldn't." Hands on hips, she planted her feet wide and jutted her chin.

"Right. But stubbornness will take you only so far."

"You may scoff, but in spite of my delicate and ladylike appearance, I'm strong. Before my marriage, I worked the hacienda alongside my father's men."

"I don't doubt it, but you lived a pampered existence as Montrose's wife for eight years."

Her lips pursed. "Pampered—hardly. More like restricted."

"My point." He wanted to kiss her pouty mouth, but that would only delay their digging out. "Come on." He tugged on the rope, testing the strength. "That should hold."

His breath hung in the air. A hard shiver passed through his body. Colder than it was last night. Damn, they needed to get back to a substantial shelter. And fast. He walked over to the gable door and tossed the rope bale onto the snow. It sank into the drifts. No time like the present.

With Talia peeking over his shoulder, he said, "Wait until I'm on the ground, then toss me the shovels. You can follow me after that."

She nodded her agreement, then said, "Be careful. I'm not very good at setting broken bones."

"Hmph." He inventoried her slight frame. Her raven-black hair was pulled back and bound with a length of twine, her eyes bright with excitement. In spite of all her claims of strength, and while the woman might be a demanding tiger in bed, she was slender and carried an air of fragility about her. Yet he'd felt her strength. Enjoyed it to the fullest. Mouth suddenly dry, he swallowed. "Worry about your own bones." His words came out with a rasp and sounded gruffer than he intended.

Damn. She was getting to him on a level he'd never expected. Never wanted. Without another word, he took the rope in his gloved hands, then sat on the floor with his feet and legs outside the gable door. Wrapping his legs around the rope, he eased outside. The wind buffeted his body around, knocking him into the side of the stable. Son of a bitch. He grunted, then started working his way down the rope.

As soon as his boots reached the level of the snow, he released his hold on the rope, dropping into a chest-high drift. He struggled and kept on his feet. "Okay, throw 'em down." He ducked as she tossed one shovel then the other a little too close to his head. "Trying to kill me?"

Her response was a light-hearted giggle. Guess she still didn't realize how much trouble they were in—as in deepest shit.

"Watch out!" she called, then launched from the gable, sliding down the rope as nimbly as if she'd done it every day of her life.

Jared grabbed the rope to stabilize it and keep the wind from slamming her into the side of the stable. He caught her around the waist and set her on her feet.

She smiled up at him, her dark eyes shining with mischief. "*Gracias.*" She pulled the heavy coat tighter and gave a visible shiver. "Brr. It's really cold—worse than I thought."

He shook his head and handed her a shovel. "No time to

waste or we'll be spending another night in the stable."

She took the shovel, gazing at him over the handle. "Now that wouldn't be so bad—would it?" Her dark lashes fluttered. "All in all, I was very comfortable"—she paused, then added—"in your arms."

"Talia, cut it out." He turned from her and attacked the drift in front of the stable. "First...things...first." He shoveled, emphasizing each word. "Clear enough to open the door and squeeze through."

"*Sí, jefe.*" Her shoulders drooped, but finally she put her shovel to furious use, sending snow flying everywhere.

"Pace yourself," he warned. "Might not make it all the way to the ranch house today." His stomach rumbled, reminding him neither of them had eaten since dinner the night before. Another night in the stable would mean another twenty-four hours without anything but fresh milk, but he'd much rather get Talia back to the house.

Chapter Eight

"Really?" Natalia's stomach growled. "I'm starving."

He glared over his shoulder. "If you hadn't been so damned determined to venture out into the storm, you could've remained inside, reasonably warm and well-fed."

"You *ordered* me to stay inside. I don't like being ordered to do anything. Besides, I was worried...and everything turned out all right, didn't it?" If "all right" meant the fucking of her life, then yes, indeed it had. She smiled up at him, feeling her cheeks grow warm from the memory of his lovemaking.

"Shovel. Now."

She bit back an equally abrupt response and set her back to tackling the deep snow. Apparently, *he* had a short memory. Last night meant nothing to him. Why would it? She was just a lonely widow he most likely intended to separate from her money. And what was he to her? Nothing more than a welcome respite from the neglect and disdain to which she'd become accustomed as the wife of Reginald Cabot Montrose.

Still, she could envision a future with Jared, working side-by-side with him. Even if he was a stranger, he was more of a partner than Reginald had ever been.

She shook off the notion of a future with anyone. Never again would she be under some man's thumb. Now that she had Reginald's money and her family's land back under her control, she had power. The power to do whatever, whenever, and with whomever she wanted. Now, that was true power—like that of a man. And she wouldn't be surrendering it to anyone.

Let alone an arrogant stranger who fucked like a steam-powered machine.

Hours later—no, maybe it was months later—Jared lifted the final shovelful of snow. He tugged on the ranch house's kitchen door until it opened. The night sky was darkening quickly, and the howling of the wind had increased in intensity. With his arm around Talia's slender waist, he literally dragged her inside the cold, dark house. At least they were out of the wind.

He carried the exhausted Talia to her bedroom, then laid her on the chaise. He covered her shivering body with a quilted coverlet from the bed. *Have to see about removing her wet clothing later. First, a fire.*

Kneeling before the fireplace, he found a small stack of mesquite, enough to start a decent fire, but it wouldn't last them through another long night.

Once the fire caught, he stood. Talia appeared to be asleep. No wonder; she'd worked as hard as any man, but the cold wind had sapped her strength during the final hour of their ordeal. He lit a lamp to chase away the gathering darkness, then walked over to her wardrobe and opened it. Nothing but useless dresses of silk and lace. What she needed next to her skin was dry undergarments and layers of clothing.

He shivered. Matter of fact, warm anything would feel pretty good right now. Raiding Montrose's wardrobe could wait. Getting Talia dry came first. He walked over to an ornately carved walnut chest situated at the foot of her bed. The chest appeared old enough to have come off a boat from Spain and been handed down through the generations. Maybe she'd brought it with her as part of her dowry. He opened the wood-and-brass closure and lifted the lid.

He smiled. Very fine woolen underwear, fit for a rich man's wife. Apparently, Montrose spared no expense for his wife's clothes. Might still be alive if he'd paid less attention to her attire and more to her other needs. Taking two pairs of everything, Jared set the undergarments on her bed.

He pulled the chaise closer to the fire, then sat beside her, stroking the side of her face. "Talia?" Her skin was pale and remained cool to his touch. Fear built in his chest. Fear he hadn't gotten her inside quickly enough. "Talia!"

Her dark lashes fluttered; then she opened her eyes. Taking a ragged breath, she gazed around the room, appearing dazed. "I—when did we...?"

"Shh. You weren't quite as strong as you thought. Had to drag you the last few yards. That's all." He gave a casual shrug as if it weren't an issue of life and death. What was the point in letting her know how he'd panicked when she'd faltered? How he'd dug frantically, like a madman, until he cleared the final path to safety.

"Sorry to have been a burden." Letting out a small sigh, she scooted up on her elbows. "The fire feels wonderful. I don't know when I've ever been so cold."

"Let's get you changed into some dry clothes." He glanced over at the Spanish chest. "I found some, uh, *things* and set them on your bed. The more layers you wear, the better." Strange he should feel any embarrassment when it came to naming her unmentionables. Not after the night they'd spent together. Still, this was her bedroom. Her home. And he was little more than a stranger.

No, he was a Pinkerton agent with an assignment. Best remember that.

Laughing, Natalia reached to unbutton his coat and shirt, snaked her arms around his waist, then rested her cheek on his bare chest. "Let's get you changed as well."

He sucked in a breath. The warmth of her exhalations against his skin sent shivers up his spine. He pressed a kiss on top of her head and shut his eyes as he held her. In his mind's eye, he could see the two of them together...forever. What sweeter comfort could any man find than in the arms of this woman?

The burning mesquite popped, reminding him of the need for more firewood. "I'll change, but I need to go back out for more wood, and it's already time to feed the horses."

"Really? I can't believe it took so long. Wait. I'll go with you." She sat straight up. "Won't take as long."

He shook his head. "No, you almost didn't make it last time. I know you don't like taking orders, but this time, you *must* stay inside the house. With the trench and the rope for a guide, I won't be gone long."

Her dark eyes widened, flashing with fiery rebellion. "I'm going!"

"No, you're not. If I have to tie you down, I will."

"Then I'd be your prisoner instead of Reginald's." Her expression grew pensive as she stuck the tip of her forefinger in her mouth and sucked. "I might not mind being *yours*."

He gazed into the darkest of brown eyes. "Promise me."

"I promise." Her words were what he wanted to hear, but her tone held a note of vacillation.

"You mean it? You'll stay inside?"

"*Sí*."

"You won't leave the house for any reason. No matter what. None."

"*Sí. Sí. Sí!*" She pummeled his chest lightly. "But you are such a stubborn man."

"I'm not the stubborn one." He shook his head. The woman would drive him mad if he let her. "That's you."

"And if I were not, we wouldn't have spent such an interesting evening."

He stood and stepped away from the fire...and Talia, lest he get burned. Damn. Best get out of the lady's reach. "There would've been no need for an 'interesting evening' had you remained inside as instructed."

Sticking her nose in the air, she gave a little huff. "Was making love to me such a chore, Jared?"

"Not a chore, but it wouldn't have happened otherwise." It shouldn't have happened at all, but she was freezing...and he was a man. Enough said.

"I beg to disagree." She gave an arrogant toss of her

hair. Her long black locks were in disarray from the day's work. "It was going to happen—one way or another."

"You're awfully certain of your allure, *señora*." Even in the soggy, shapeless clothes she wore, she was more than alluring. His cock was hard as a brick. He wanted nothing more than to loosen the rest of her hair and carry her to the bed and make love to her all over again.

Her sensual mouth pulled into a catlike smile as she shot him a sideways glance. "A woman knows when she's desired." She rose from the chaise and started removing her wet garments. Unbuttoning the flannel shirt slowly—one button at a time—she revealed the silken skin he already knew so well.

"From the first time we met, I knew you wanted me." Her dark gaze held him immobile. He wanted to look away but couldn't. Mouth dry, he swallowed.

"You couldn't hide your interest any more than my husband could hide his lack." She shrugged off the shirt, then nimbly stepped out of the wet denims. Like some sort of wild-animal mating ritual, she preened, caressing the curves of her body in the light of the fire. "Any more than you can hide your desire now." Her knowing gaze dropped to his crotch.

Fearful of losing all control, he turned away. "For God's sake, Natalia. Please get dressed before you freeze to death. You know I need to go back and feed the animals." Unwilling to give in to her sensual power, he strode from the room.

*

Dios! How dare he leave her naked and alone? Natalia called after him, "You would've frozen to death with nothing but two horses and a cow for company." She stomped her foot, but it did nothing to relieve her frustration. What an infuriating man—just when she thought she had his undivided attention. But as much as she hated to admit it, he was right to consider the creatures that couldn't fend for themselves.

While she dreaded leaving the meager heat emanating from the fire, she might as well get dressed. Her stomach growled again. First warm clothes, then food.

She quickly pulled on the woolen underwear, then found another pair of heavy denim pants and stepped into them. After buttoning them, she pulled not just one but two plaid flannel shirts from the chifforobe drawer. Two layers of everything. That should be sufficient to keep from freezing and still be able to walk around. The flannel shirts were soft and warm against her skin, and finally she was able to stop shivering.

To hell with Jared Fields for his offhand manner. She could hear him rummaging around in Reginald's bedroom. Fortunately, Sarita hadn't had time to get rid of his old clothes.

At the thought of Sarita, tears welled in Natalia's eyes. Surely her housekeeper and friend had made it to her husband and their snug little house before the snowstorm worsened. There was nothing Natalia could do now. But as soon as the weather cleared enough, she would saddle her mare and ride over to their cabin.

In the meantime, Natalia was so hungry it felt like her belly was rubbing against her backbone. She strode down the central hall, meaning to head for the kitchen, but Jared suddenly emerged from Reginald's bedchamber. He set his hands on her shoulders, blocking her way. Damn him! She stepped back and gave him a none-too-gentle shove. "Out of my way."

"Where do you think you're off to now?" One dark brow arched as if he was amused by her action.

She glared up at him, torn between smacking his bristly cheek or kissing it. "The kitchen. Am I the only one who's hungry?" She stepped to the side, aiming to go around him, but he matched her step in a smooth waltz-like glide. Pulling her into his arms, he held her tight against his chest and spun her around.

"Stop it. This isn't one of your fancy cotillion balls. Besides, you're still damp." But his nearness was getting to her, if her weakening knees and ragged breathing were indications. "Go change," she said with a softening of her tone. "I'll fix us something to eat."

"Talia..." His voice deepened and broke. "I could eat you all night and all day for that matter." He ducked his head, then said, "Sorry I snapped. You have a way of throwing me off balance."

Shooting him a warm glance, she curtsied. "Of course, *Señor* Fields. That's been my plan all along." The thought of his tongue and how it felt sliding wetly between her legs sent a shudder through her body. Smiling and in grave danger of losing herself in his dark steel gaze, she shook her head. "Soon, *that* would not be enough. Eventually, we would die of starvation."

A merry laugh erupted from the man who still held her in his arms. "Might have a point at that." He released her after planting a quick kiss on her forehead. "I'll change. But then I'm heading out again... The animals. Firewood, remember?"

"Yes, firewood, unless you want cold stew."

"I've eaten worse." He grinned down at her, his gray eyes shining with good humor. "But I do prefer my meat—uh, meals—hot."

"Then get the firewood, and I'll see to it that everything you eat"—pausing, she fluttered her lashes for effect—"is just the way you like it."

"Your kindness and consideration are much appreciated, ma'am." The cheeky bastard winked, bowed, then returned to Reginald's bedchamber to change into dry clothes.

Yes, his meaning was clear. Tonight would be another night for fucking. And it would be in the comfort of her bed, not on top of a smelly, scratchy horse blanket placed on a pile of hay. The thought sent a curl of pleasure to her belly and below. Clamping her knees together, she squirmed.

He'd better hurry with that firewood. She couldn't wait much longer.

Once in the kitchen, Natalia checked the icebox, Reginald's last extravagant purchase before meeting his demise. Sarita had saved the remaining portion of the stew in a covered saucepan. Natalia lifted the lid and saw there was enough for another meal. Next she lit a candle and carried it into the pantry. The shelves were lined with glass jars of dried beans and canned tomatoes from the hacienda's small garden, as well as a variety of tinned food items purchased in the town's small general store. Reginald had been very fond of his food, and what couldn't be bought locally, he ordered in quantity from stores back East. Dried chilies were stored according to variety in a rectangular, covered tin pan. Thanks to Sarita's hard work, the root section of the wine cellar was well stocked with potatoes, sweet potatoes, onions and even apples from the handful of trees Reginald insisted on planting.

In other words, thanks to Reginald's love of food, they weren't in danger of starving. But what about her ranch hands and the two thousand head of cattle waiting in town to go to market? If the snow didn't end soon, many would be lost. Perhaps all.

In the meantime, there was nothing she could do except survive.

She walked back into the kitchen and found Jared there, warmly dressed in her late but not lamented husband's old clothes and prepared to go back into the storm. Reginald's clothes fit Jared's lean-hipped body loosely, but he looked handsome nonetheless.

"As you suggested, I helped myself."

"He won't mind where he is. Hell, I hope. I was going to have Sarita burn them, but then it occurred to me that we should distribute everything to those who were in need. I suppose this qualifies."

He glanced down at the leather belt holding up his baggy trousers. "It does."

She reached up to caress his dark, bristled cheek and smiled. "As you can see, Reginald was *very* fond of his food. He would've called you a poor specimen of a man."

"No doubt." He nodded his agreement. "Too much time on horseback and too little at fine dinner tables."

She took his calloused hands in hers, still gazing into his steely eyes. "However, I do not."

His arms went around her waist, pulling her close. Her lower body connected with his, making the hard jut of his cock impossible to miss. Molded so close to him, she could feel every beat of his heart. He dipped his head and slanted his mouth over hers. She parted her lips to the fevered assault of his tongue. Her knees began to feel as mushy as overcooked rice.

As she was about to rip open his shirt, he stopped kissing her and pulled away. "Later."

"Later?" she asked, still dazed by the onslaught of desire ripping through her entire body.

"Firewood." He kissed the tip of her nose. "Food." He kissed her neck and moved down to nuzzle her breasts through the thick flannel shirts. Meeting her gaze again, he added, "Then, dear Talia, fucking."

His frank language made her inner muscles clench. Unable to hold back a nervous chuckle, she said, "At least *your* priorities are in order. It's good to know where I stand." She reached for his collar, pulling it tighter around his neck. "Be careful. I think the wind has picked up, so you shouldn't stay outside any longer than necessary." Shivering, she rubbed her upper arms.

He grinned down at her, slipping a stray lock of hair behind her ear. "Careful, Talia. Your maternal side is showing."

She smiled, loving the husky sound of her name on Jared's lips. Old Reginald had insisted on calling her

"Nata-*lee*" rather than by her true name and correct pronunciation. "I'm not sure my maternal instincts have ever been tested before. And I'm not sure they ever will." No, she would never marry again. Never give up her land, her power or her heart.

"There's definitely a maternal side to you. Of that I have no doubt."

"Go." She shivered and rubbed her arms. "But don't stay too long. I'm starving." In more ways than one.

"Me too," he said with a wink and a nod. Then, pulling his coat collar tighter, he turned and eased out the kitchen door into the night.

Still quivering, Natalia stood in the door, watching until he was lost in the dark and howling wind. She eased the door closed. Hopefully the snow hadn't drifted so much that the trench they'd dug had filled in. Plus he had the rope to use as a guide back to the stables. He wouldn't get lost in the blizzard. He wouldn't.

No matter who or what Jared really was didn't matter. What did matter was that she didn't have to spend the rest of the winter snowed in...and alone.

For now, she would take advantage of all Jared's skills...in and out of bed. And after he left, she'd be alone again. When Reginald was killed, she confessed she'd been more than relieved. She'd been grateful he no longer had control of her body and life, but now being alone didn't have quite the same appeal. If she was honest, she'd miss Jared's strength and his company.

Chapter Nine

After caring for the two horses and the cow, Jared shut the stable door. There was plenty of feed, but water was in short supply, unless he could melt some of the damned snow. As he headed around the side of the stable to where Talia said the firewood was located, his footsteps crunched through the deep snow. The path he and Talia had dug was still passable, and the rope remained a secure guide for traveling to and from the house to the stable a hundred yards away. And for the moment, the wind had stopped blowing. Instead of blinding horizontal sweeps of the white stuff, snow now drifted down softly in fat flakes. There was no moon. The silence was eerie. As far as he could see, there was nothing but snow and the snow-covered humps of the other ranch outbuildings.

Using leather strips and a couple of wood planks he'd found in the stable, he fashioned a small travois-like contraption he could use to drag a supply of wood back to the ranch house. All he had to do now was clear another path to find the woodpile. Holding back a groan, he stopped long enough to stretch his neck and back muscles, already aching from the day's digging...and maybe last night's exertions in keeping Talia from freezing to death. The thought of her waiting for his return brought a smile to his face. What were a few more hours of backbreaking work? The sooner he started, the sooner he could pull her into his arms.

By the light of a kerosene lamp, Talia paced. A myriad of worries flashed through her mind. Jared had been gone for what seemed like hours. Had he fallen? Been injured? Maybe the woodpile collapsed on top of him? Should she risk going out again to find him? That particular strategy hadn't worked too well last time. She was the one who fell and nearly froze to death before he rescued her. Maybe this time, he was the one in need of rescue.

She turned to go to her bedroom for more clothes. The rattle of the door caught her attention; she spun to find Jared's tall frame silhouetted in the doorway. A wave of relief rushed through her as she ran to him and threw her arms around his neck. "You're all right. I was so worried."

He brushed the snow from his Stetson. "Cold. And hungry. But I'm all right."

He pulled her closer and covered her mouth with his, kissing her like a man starved and thirsting for more of her love. She opened her mouth to his, and as she did, her stomach growled loudly. Laughing, they broke apart. "*Dios*," she said, "how rude of me."

"You're hungry too." He grinned and glanced toward the door. "There's a good supply of wood. Couple of days' worth."

"Good." She smiled at the thought of being warm again.

"I'll build the fire in the cookstove, if you'll tend to the fireplaces."

He nodded, leveling his steely gaze on her. "Best we conserve the wood and only use *one* of the fireplaces."

She assumed her most wide-eyed expression of innocence. "Then I suggest we use the one in my bedchamber."

"My thoughts exactly." His voice was low and husky, sending a shiver of desire running through her body.

She smiled up at him. His eyes glittered with a sensual lust, but there were dark circles beneath telling her just how exhausted he was from the day's exertions. As for her own flagging spirits, the sight of the firewood energized her.

He cleared his throat. "I'd—uh, better carry a couple of logs into your room, then."

"Yes, do that." She worried her bottom lip with her teeth. Soon they would have the remainder of the rich beef stew to eat and the Rioja to quench their thirsts.

And afterwards they would lie down skin to skin in the soft comfort of her featherbed and make love until the sun rose. Making love with Jared was a revelation. He gave her immeasurable pleasure without asking in return, but tonight she would pleasure him.

She hummed a little tune while she laid the fire in the cookstove. After the wood caught, she held her hands over the stove, relishing the warmth that had begun to emanate. Fortunately, Sarita had taught her everything she needed to know about managing a house and cooking. Everything she needed to know to be a good wife to her husband. Unfortunately, her father had married her off to a man who neither loved nor respected her. But now with Jared, maybe she had another chance at happiness.

No! Thoughts like those were dangerous. Risking her heart, not to mention her newly inherited fortune, was reckless. Never again would she allow a man to control her life...or her money. And wasn't that what men did? It was part and parcel of their gender to crave power and control. This time she would be the one with all the power over her holdings.

She looked down at her clenched fists. Forcing her fingers to relax, she took in a deep breath.

A hand landed on her shoulder. She jumped, so intent on her thoughts she hadn't heard Jared's approach. "*Madre de Dios!*"

"Pardon. I didn't mean to startle you," Jared said. "Are you all right?"

"Fine." She drew her slightly trembling hands back through her hair, smoothing it away from her forehead. "You *did* startle me. My fault, though. I fear my mind was elsewhere."

"May I help?" His dark brows pulled together in a frown. One corner of his mustache twitched.

She held back a laugh. Her thoughts had surprised her and taken her into dark territory. Not Jared's fault at all, but he certainly appeared guilty, as if he'd done something to displease her.

"If you'll take the leftover stew from the icebox, I think the stove is hot enough. I'll set the table."

She watched as he crouched and removed the pot of stew. "I'm glad we didn't eat it all last night. It was last night, wasn't it? I'm afraid I've lost track of time. Honestly, it feels like it was a week ago." *Dios*, why must she babble so?

"Yes. Early yesterday evening." He set the pot on the stove plate. "We had rather a late evening." This time, the corner of his mouth twisted upward in a wry smile.

Grinning up at him, Talia removed the lid and stirred the stew with a large wooden spoon. "And it appears as if we might be in for another one."

"Sounds as if the lady has something in mind— something besides digging another trench in the snow." He eased behind her, spanning her waist with his large hands while he placed soft kisses up and down the side of her neck. "I will be happy to oblige but won't presume to know the intricacies of female desires."

She smiled to herself and kept stirring the stew. "And here I have the singular notion that you're very aware of a woman's desires—especially those of this particular woman." With that, she turned to face him, snaking her arms around his waist, their bodies now so close she could feel his cock harden against her belly. "It seems a man's desires are much more evident and more difficult to hide."

"So it would seem." She felt him shudder. Was he rocked by lust as she was? Was the weakness in her legs the result of longing or the fact she hadn't eaten in over twenty-four hours? She sagged against him, her head beginning to spin. Black splotches marred her vision.

"Talia!" Alarmed by her sudden pale face and collapse, Jared caught her before she fell. "Talia..." He scooped her up, carried her across the kitchen and settled her gently onto one of the rugged wood chairs.

Her lids fluttered, then opened wide as she gazed around the kitchen. "What happened?"

"You swooned."

"Don't be absurd." She raised her chin like a haughty society *grande dame*. "I'm not some silly debutante from the East. I *never* swoon."

His mouth twitched with a smile. "Maybe not, but you did all the same." He crossed the kitchen to the cookstove. "You have to eat. Now."

She tried to rise, but faltered and sat back with a sigh.

Damned stubborn woman. "Just sit. I can dish up a bowl of stew." He grabbed two bowls from the table, then took them back to the stove where the thick, meaty stew was beginning to bubble. His mouth watered. Ignoring his hunger, he removed the pot from the fire and set it aside.

She nodded, then pointed. "There's a loaf of bread in the keeper. It only needs to be sliced."

"One thing at a time." He held up both hands. "I only have two of these."

Talia laughed. "Men."

He scrambled to the bread-keeper and pulled out a fragrant loaf. "Knife? Butter?"

She nodded toward a table along the side of the kitchen. "Blue round crock...the one with a lid. Knives are kept in a wooden block," she said, waving with an elegant gesture, "in that drawer."

He snatched the butter-keeper with one hand and opened the knife drawer with the other. He set the crock on the table in front of Talia, then cut her a thick slice of bread. "Eat that while I dish up your stew." Damn. His stomach felt so empty it had to be collapsed on itself.

Mouth watering, he watched while she slathered butter on the bread. She stuffed a portion in her mouth, making a mewing noise of satisfaction.

"You—eat," she said, pointing at him. Though her words were muffled due to her mouthful of bread, her intention was clear.

"Right." He turned and quickly ladled stew into the two bowls, then pulled out a chair and sat. He took a quick bite and burned his tongue. No matter. Hunger definitely enhanced the flavor. "Delicious," he muttered, trying to keep from wolfing down the spicy stew. The bread was fresh, its texture thick, and the taste of yeast overwhelmed him. God. Almost starved and didn't know it. He could've eaten the entire loaf himself, not to mention the entire pot of stew.

While he was stuffing his face, he watched Talia eat. Once she'd consumed half a slice of bread, she recovered her ladylike manners, and while it was obvious she was enjoying her first meal in twenty-four hours, she hadn't descended to eating like a pig at the trough as he had.

Once he'd finished his second bowl of stew, he groaned and pushed back from the table. "Sorry. Once I started, I couldn't stop."

Dark eyes glowing, she smiled, showing a deep dimple on one side of her beautiful face. How had he not noticed that sweet dip before?

"I like to see a man enjoy his dinner. Even such simple fare as this."

"I've not enjoyed any meal as much as this one, not in any fine dining room in all of New York City."

"You have Sarita to think for our wonderful meal." Her

expression grew cloudy. "Do you think she made it home in time?" Her voice caught. "I can't bear to think of her lying out there, buried somewhere in the snowstorm. Frozen like I almost..."

He caught her hand and held it to his lips. "I'm sure she made it to shelter." A small lie to comfort Talia, but not impossible. "Or she would've turned back."

Her luminous gaze pierced his heart. "Do you really think so?"

"I do." At best, the older woman had a fifty-fifty chance of making it a half mile in one of the worst snowstorms he'd ever seen. Being he was a gambler at heart, he'd want better odds if he was going to place a bet on the woman's survival. He rose from his chair and walked around the well-scrubbed pine table to where Talia sat. Pulling her to her feet, he enfolded her in his arms, then rested his head on hers. He emitted a bark of laughter. "You have straw in your hair." He removed it gently and held it out so she could see.

She bit her full bottom lip and giggled. "I can't imagine where I must've picked that up. Can you?"

"No. Not at all. But if you're not careful, someone will see it and think you're a woman of loose morals who tumbles in the hay with regularity."

"I'm shocked. No one would believe it of me. Certainly not any of the strumpets frequented by dear old Reginald."

Without thinking, they stood and left the warmth of the cozy kitchen, then headed down a much cooler hallway. "Cannot understand why your late husband would require their services. Not with a woman like you in his bed."

"I didn't understand it either, but he preferred others to

me. Not that I found him particularly desirable."

"What was he like, this husband of yours?"

"He was about your height but much heavier through the middle. Not from muscle but from too many rich dinners. Quite imposing. He wore his air of superiority like a fine suit of clothes. It was never more evident than when he came in contact with the locals, especially me. I was merely the Mexican slut he married as part of the bargain to gain my family's land and cattle."

Jared swore under his breath, pulling her lush body closer, inhaling her unique scent. "There's no explaining fools," he said. "You're a beautiful and passionate woman. Any man with brains enough to keep his head from collapsing would count himself fortunate beyond words to have a woman like you." Damnation. What was he saying? While every word was true, he needn't have made it sound like a declaration of love. His peripatetic life wasn't suitable for a wife. Not that he'd ever considered marriage...with anyone.

"Then you, sir, are obviously a man of great intelligence—nay, wisdom."

"I've made a lot of mistakes in my life, but I know a hell of a woman when I see one." And the thought of digging into the death of her thankless husband appealed less and less with each passing second. The true crime was neglecting Talia and treating her with anything less than the respect she deserved.

They reached the door to her bedchamber. She leaned against the doorjamb and gazed up at him. "I'll adjust the fire," he said, "and wish you good evening."

The tiniest of frowns flitted across her face, followed by

a smug grin. "Yes and no."

"What?" No, he wasn't confused, but neither did he assume the lady would share her body and bed with him for a second night. No matter how much he desired her. No matter how hard his cock.

She eased into her room. "Yes, bank the fire, but you're not going anywhere," she said with a haughty glance over her shoulder.

What else could he do? He followed. "I confess I hoped you wouldn't send me away."

"We have to conserve the firewood—you said as much yourself." She dimpled at him again, adding a sweet expression of innocence to her beautiful face. "Stands to reason we'll be warmer sleeping together."

"You make a convincing argument." He knelt in front of the fire, using the poker to turn over one of the mesquite logs for better burning.

"Even if we don't sleep much?" Her suggestive tone caused his head to turn. Lord, she was unbuttoning her shirt.

His mouth grew dry. "Not a half hour ago, you nearly passed out from lack of food and rest."

She shrugged off the two layers of flannel, leaving her upper body clad only in the fine woolen underwear which outlined her lush breasts and hard nipples. "*I* feel quite refreshed."

"As do I." He rose and closed the distance between them. He cupped her full breasts through the wool. Her nipples were already tightened into small pearls. She reached down and grabbed the hem of the garment and whipped it over her head, exposing the beauty of her breasts to his gaze. He caressed her silken skin, circling the dark areolas with his thumbs. Already his prick felt as if it might burst at the slightest touch.

He dipped his head to lick one of the dark nubs, then teased it with a gentle rake of his teeth.

Arching her back and thrusting her breasts forward, she gasped, "*Sí*, more." He picked her up and carried her to the bed. Pulling back the counterpane, he laid her gently on the bed. She reached to unbutton her denim trousers. Always the gentleman, he offered his assistance by helping her wiggle out of them, then tossed them aside.

Next came her woolen drawers. Slowly sliding them from under her round bottom, then down her long shapely legs, he sucked in a breath when he revealed the dark patch at the apex of her thighs. Talia was more beautiful than any woman he'd ever had. And he'd had more than a few. From hurried caresses with society debutants to a scandalous liaison with a stage actress and a soiled dove or two, he'd never lacked for female companionship. But it had been months since his last opportunity. Perhaps that was why his response to Talia was so strong.

She squirmed up toward the head of the bed and assumed a seductive position. Gazing up at him, her smoldering eyes caught the glow of the fire. "You're next. In the stable, all I could do was *feel* your body. Now, I want to see all of you." Smiling, she patted the bed beside her.

He nodded, quickly shucking his clothing until the garments lay in a pile at his feet. With a shiver as the room's cold air hit his skin, he jumped into the bed and snatched up the counterpane. "It's cold in here."

"Not for long," she said, smiling, her voice rich with the

promise of what was to come. As she scooted close to him, the heat of her breasts warmed his chest. One of her legs entwined with his, bringing the damp heat of her pussy to writhe against his thigh. God.

"You are quite beautiful. '*Muy* handsome', as Sarita would say."

"Men aren't beautiful." He shook his head. "Our bodies are nothing compared to the softness and fragrance of a woman's. *You* are beautiful, Talia. I'm merely the lucky man with whom you've chosen to share that loveliness." Damnation. He had a job to do, and here he was, sounding more like a poet than a Pinkerton.

Careful, you're in danger of losing yourself in the depths of her eyes.

With a smile of seeming satisfaction, she arched her neck, offering him the temptation to sample her soft skin. What else could he do? He planted kisses along the slender column, then nibbled her ear and finished with a quick nip of the tender lobe. Wisps of silken tresses lay in strands on her neck. He reached to loosen her hair, and it fell in a dark mass of waves on her pillow.

"I think you like using your teeth on me," she murmured. "I like it too." She nipped his ear, certainly harder than he had hers.

"Ouch. Careful or I'll leave my mark on you," he said.

"You've already left your mark on me. I'll never be the same."

He fastened his mouth on her neck and sucked until a red love bite was visible. "Now you're marked. *And* you're mine." *For now, anyway.*

Talia laughed. "That works both ways." She rolled until

she was on top of him. His curiosity about what she would do next was quickly answered. She leaned forward and kissed his nipple. He'd never considered how sensitive they were until she fastened on to one and sucked.

He groaned from the intensity of sensation that arrowed straight to his cock. "There, now *you're* marked." This time, she giggled and left a trail of kisses from his chest down to his abdomen. Raising her head, she gazed down at him. "But I think I'd rather mark you somewhere else."

Jared's cock was already standing at attention and couldn't possibly get any harder. Or so he thought. He craved her touch and a sweet release. He felt the wet warmth of her tongue flicking the head of his dick.

Startled, he sucked in a breath. Then she took him inside her mouth, her tongue swirling around the head, licking him. Bobbing her head over his staff, she sucked.

Dear God. Each of her movements brought him excruciating pleasure. His body heated; his balls throbbed until they contracted. He threw his head back and groaned, his climax blasting through his entire body. His hips arching, he drove helplessly into her mouth as cum spurted from his cock.

Unbelievably, she took all of him, even swallowing his emissions. He gasped for air, trying to apologize. "Sorry. No time. Didn't mean..."

She gazed up at him from her position between his thighs. "I meant for that to happen. Tonight was about pleasuring you."

"Not like I wasn't pleasured before. Come here." He reached under her arms and pulled her up to his chest. "That was unbelievable." Indeed, she gave head as if she'd done it for a living. Doubts about her crept unwanted into his mind.

"Reginald..." Her cheeks darkened, and she averted her gaze as if suddenly embarrassed. "That's what he preferred..."

"But gave no thought to your pleasure?" *The bastard.*

She shook her head, her dark hair shining like silk in the firelight. "No. I told you, to him I was a Mexican whore, even though I was a virgin when we married. After the first night, he never touched me that way again."

Ashamed for doubting her, Jared gently brushed back the hair from her forehead. "Such a waste," he said, shaking his head in disbelief. How any man reared in a genteel, upper-class East Coast family could treat any woman in such an ungentlemanly manner, especially this one, was a mystery.

She gazed at him earnestly, her bottom lip trembling. How could he not read the truth in those sad eyes?

"You'll think less of me," she said with a sigh, "but I'll risk telling you this anyway."

"Go on." He kissed the sweet spot below her ear and felt his cock begin to stir.

"At the burial, I swore on his very grave I would bed the first clean and available man I ran across."

Yes, he could imagine her doing that very thing. "Lucky me." He cupped both breasts and kissed them. Did she have any idea of the effect she had on him? Her woman's scent alone was driving him crazy. Let her talk. He wanted to prolong every moment he spent with her.

"No." She caressed his cheek. "I am the fortunate one. Not only have you been thoughtful about my—uh, womanly needs"—she grinned, showing that single deep dimple again—"you saved my life. I can't imagine what hell going through this snowstorm would be without you."

He stopped the breast play and leveled his gaze at her. Keeping his tone matter-of-fact, he said, "You strike me as a very capable woman, Talia. You would've survived." Though given her propensity for rash action, he wasn't sure he believed his own words.

"*Sí*, but it wouldn't have been nearly so interesting or enjoyable." She wriggled against his cock.

Holding back a groan of pleasure, he amended his earlier statement through gritted teeth. "That is, you would've survived, as long as you stayed in the ranch house."

"But I wouldn't have. I would've seen after my mare, and I wouldn't let the cow suffer, either." She smiled down at him as she moved her pelvis sensuously against his.

It was time for him to surrender. She wasn't going to. "Then it's true. I came along at the right time; otherwise, you would've certainly died."

"But you did, and I did not." Talia dipped her head, opening her full lips for an assault on his mouth. Her tongue battled with his while she slipped her hand between their bodies and found his cock.

Startled by her bold handling, he sucked in a quick breath and tried to rein in the impulse to let go. "I've never known anyone like you." Indeed, never had any woman left him wanting more and more of her love. And no woman had ever made him consider spending a lifetime in her arms. "God, woman, you're killing me."

Chapter Ten

Natalia threw her head back and laughed. "That wouldn't serve any useful purpose, now would it?" Without waiting for a reply, she straddled him. His cock was already hard again. Rubbing the head up and down her wet slit, she luxuriated in the sweet sensations the mere touch of it sent curling through her body.

"That feels good, does it?" he murmured.

"Ever so good."

"What about this?" He brought one of her breasts to his mouth and sucked the nipple into a tight nub, then rolled it back and forth over his teeth. Her inner walls contracted with the exquisite burst of sensation that centered in her lower belly. Grasping his thick cock firmly, she positioned her body over it and slid just the head inside her pussy. Gripping his shoulders, she eased down onto his hard shaft.

She gasped as the length and breadth of it filled her. While she remained tender from their earlier lovemaking, her body quickly adjusted to his size. Slowly, she began to move, rocking back and forth as if he were a newly purchased mount. Straightening her back, she cupped her breasts and tweaked her nipples. Jared smiled up at her, grasped her waist with his large hands while he bucked upward, matching her rhythm. Each stroke took him deeper and deeper into her core and into her soul.

Her body warmed with their efforts, and perspiration began to bead on her forehead. He pulled her forward until her breasts rested softly against his chest, and increased the pace. Their bellies slapped together wetly. Her breathing grew ragged, and she felt as if she were on fire. *Dios*, she was desperate to come. "Faster. Faster," she gasped. Jared thrust into her as if his hips were driven by pistons, his breathing as labored as hers.

"Come for me, Talia. Come for me." He gave a last mighty stroke and groaned. The world around her disappeared, and they flew over the crest together, her body melding around and holding his until they could move no more.

Calling his name, she collapsed on his chest with a moan.

He kissed her neck, then her mouth, sweet, deep soul kisses. Kisses she would never forget. Never, as long as she lived.

She licked the sweat from his brow while he brushed back her hair, damp with perspiration. If she could lick him from head to foot, she would never need another bite to eat.

"You're so beautiful," he said. "So full of passion and life." He ran his hands down her bottom, then gave her a playful slap. "I could—"

Staring down at him, she frowned, then levered onto her elbows. "You could what?"

Jared shook his head. "Oh—uh, I could make love to you all day and night."

"*Really*?" Somehow, she knew that wasn't what he'd meant to say. He wasn't the kind of man who stammered and stuttered around. What was really on his mind? It was bad enough she was beginning to wonder what the future could be with him at her side. But no, Jared was a man with wanderlust. Whether he knew beans about financial dealings remained to be seen. Could a man like him be happy spending the rest of his life on a cattle ranch? Would he even want to?

No. Get those romantic ideas out of your head. He's a wanderer at the least and some kind of a confidence man at the worst. Either way, he'll leave you alone and heartbroken.

Jared felt Talia's body go rigid. What? "You're pulling away from me. What is it? Did I hurt you?"

"Of course not. It's nothing. I'm just suddenly very tired." She rolled over on her side, presenting him her back. "We both deserve a good night's rest," she said, her voice muffled.

"As you wish." He turned to spoon her in his arms. Her body stiffened, then relaxed bit by bit. After another minute or two, she allowed him to cup her breast. Finally, her regular breathing told him she had truly gone to sleep.

Something had changed. One minute she was wild and passionate, and the next as icy cold as one of the snow drifts outside. What was going on in the woman's head he had not a single clue. Perhaps she did have it in her to order her husband's death.

Only time would tell.

Jared eased from the bed early the next morning, setting his feet on the cold tile floor. He shivered and quickly dressed in the clothes he'd discarded so quickly last night. Talia was still asleep, her body's lush curves outlined by the quilt which was pulled up to her neck. He knelt in front of the fireplace and added more wood to the glowing embers, then lit a candle from the mantel. Getting to his feet, he checked again. Still asleep.

Time to nose around. After all, he was here for a reason, and making love to the subject of his inquiry wasn't it. However, a Pinkerton shouldn't care how he accomplished his goal, only that he did.

With another glance over his shoulder to ensure he hadn't awakened her, he opened the door to her bedchamber and closed it softly behind him. Using the candle to light his way, it didn't take long to find where the ranch's business was done. A small room located off the pantry contained a large roll-top, oak desk with a pile of ledgers. Would one of those ledgers list a payment to Juan Ojeda, the man who stabbed Reginald Montrose?

Would she be that careless? Assuming, of course, she was responsible for her husband's murder as Montrose's father believed.

He opened the top ledger and traced down the line of neat entries. The dates went back years in the same precise feminine handwriting. Apparently, Talia had kept the books for her husband long before he was killed. Not what he would have expected from someone like Montrose, a man convinced of his superiority. Perhaps he considered her as little more than an employee or servant.

Not surprising, there wasn't any record of a payment to Ojeda. While having a payment recorded would be proof positive, the absence of payment didn't prove the opposite. He closed the ledger and turned, nearly dropping the candle.

Damn.

"What are you doing?" Wrapped in the counterpane from the bed they'd shared, Talia stood in the office doorway, her brow furrowed.

He shot her his most disarming smile. "Just looking at your books. I'm a financial adviser—remember? I couldn't resist."

As regal as a queen, Talia straightened her back and lifted her chin. "Don't you usually wait for your client's permission before invading their privacy?"

"Always have." He closed the distance between them and gently slipped a silken lock of hair behind her ear. "But we don't exactly have a typical adviser-and-client relationship, now do we?"

Dark eyes blazing, she shook her head. "You presume because I shared my bed with you that I would open my books as easily as I did my legs?" Her tone matched her haughty posture, and she was clearly in no mood for his particular brand of charm.

Damn, he should have been more careful. Now to mend those fences before she tossed his ass out in the snow.

He inclined his head in the briefest of nods. "My presumption was an unforgiveable breach of conduct.

Please accept my sincerest apologies."

Talia averted her gaze, staring into the distance, as if considering whether or not to accept his apology. Abruptly, her gaze snapped back at him. "This once, I will overlook your breach of manners and accept your apology, but do not be so rash as to believe I will do so a second time."

Wrapped in the quilt, she delivered her warning with all the dignity of a queen adorned in an ermine-trimmed robe while addressing one of her errant subjects. God. What a magnificent creature. He clenched his jaw to keep from smiling. Best keep his response humble and polite. Next time, he'd be more careful.

"Thank you." He stuck his hands in his pockets and nodded. "I'll leave as soon as the weather allows."

Her eyes widened. "No!" Her cheeks darkened as if she were embarrassed by her agitated response. "I mean, we should establish some ground rules. It may be that I still require your financial advice, but only when and *if* I say so."

"Agreed." So she didn't want him to leave. "From what I saw—um, briefly, you have a good head for figures."

"My father taught me. Since he had no son and I was his only child, he felt it a necessary part of my education. While he didn't send me abroad to study as he would have a son, I had excellent tutors."

"You were very fortunate."

"In some ways, I was."

"And in other ways...?"

"My father was a volatile man, and, at times, a harsh one." Talia lifted her shoulders in a slight shrug. "Doesn't matter now, as I am my own mistress. I have the family land and cattle, as well as the responsibility that goes with them. My father lives on Reginald's gold and doesn't have a care in the world."

"Being in control is important to you, isn't it?" The real question was whether her need for control was motive enough for her to have Montrose murdered. And he still wasn't any closer to knowing the answer.

"*Sí.*"

Have to handle her carefully, since she needed to feel in control, and that need was never more evident than in bed. A passionate woman who reveled in her sensuality added a heightened factor to his enjoyment.

"What's so amusing?"

He shook his head. "What? Nothing."

"You were smiling—just a bit, but I saw it."

"I confess I was remembering how successful you are at control"—with a grin, he paused—"in other situations."

Talia flushed again, but she nodded her agreement, gazing at him with a spark of mischief lighting her ebony eyes. "*Sí,* but I don't mind relinquishing control...on occasion."

"We'll see about that...if I'm not being presumptuous again."

"Never fear. I shall let you know if you overstep."

"If Your Majesty would deign to get dressed, your subjects in the stable require our attention."

Talia's hand went to her mouth. "Right. I'll join you as soon as I've changed."

Next time, he would choose a better time for his snooping. He was damned fortunate she'd forgiven him so quickly. Either Lady Luck was on his side, or the ease with which Talia had forgiven him might mean she remained suspicious and would keep a watchful eye on his movements.

He nodded and headed back to the kitchen. "Want me to start the fire in the cookstove?"

She shook her head. "I can manage that; then I'll join you in the stable. The stove should be just right for preparing breakfast by the time we finish feeding *my subjects*."

"All right." Jared concealed what he knew. In spite of Talia's light-hearted tone, she didn't quite trust him. She was making sure he left the ranch house before she did. Not that he blamed her. There might still be some incriminating correspondence hidden in the desk. Maybe she kept a journal.

He grabbed the heavy coat from the hook. "Might as well get out there." He stepped out into the cold. The sky was beginning to lighten, but the morning sun had yet to breach the horizon. The wind blasted from the northeast. Some of the trench had filled in, but not enough to impede his quick progress to the stable.

Standing at the door, he heard the nickering of the two horses and the lowing of the cow. He kicked the small drift away from the stable door and wrenched it open. The pungent smell of manure reached his wrinkled nose. He'd have to muck the stalls today. But first he'd feed the two horses.

Natalia waited until Jared left, then locked the office door and slipped the key into her pocket. "Now for the cookstove," she muttered while she laid the fire in the stove. *Dios*. What was Jared really up to, going through her accounts in such a decidedly secretive manner? The nerve of him. Perhaps she should return the favor and rummage through his suit pockets.

Better hurry, because he expected her to follow him to the stable. She scrambled to her feet and ran to Reginald's bedroom. There. Jared's black jacket and waistcoat, made from very fine, light wool, were folded neatly over the back of a chair.

Picking the jacket up with one hand, she felt for the inside pockets with her other. Slender cigarillos were in that pocket, along with some safety matches. Nothing else of interest. She set the jacket back in its original position, then checked his waistcoat pockets. Another fruitless search. But in the bottom of an inner vest pocket, she discovered a folded telegram. Opening the telegram, she read the cryptic message, dated the same day Jared had arrived unannounced at her door.

Progress report needed [stop] Montrose anxious for result [stop]

While the message could've meant just about anything, the signer's name made her heart almost cease to beat. She grabbed the chair to steady herself.

Jasper, Pinkerton Agency

Financial adviser—hah!

Jared was a Pinkerton. *Dios mío*. She'd heard of the Pinkertons. They were ruthless thugs for hire. Was Jared investigating her? Of course he was. Why else would he be here?

Reginald's family must have hired him. But why? Surely

they didn't suspect *her* of killing him. Everyone knew Juan Ojeda and Reginald had argued over a card game, then, after Reginald went upstairs to visit one of the whores, Ojeda slipped into her room and stabbed Reginald while he was still on top of the woman.

Her heart pounded. The Montrose family must believe she'd hired Ojeda to commit murder. Jared had to be looking for proof in her office. *Bastardo*. Her hands trembled as she took great care to refold the telegram along the original creases, then replaced it in his waistcoat pocket. Taking a deep breath, she draped the garment as it was before. He must not know she'd discovered his identity.

She took another deep breath. Somehow she must calm down before she saw him again, or he'd know from her behavior she was on to him. If ever she wanted to kill someone, Jared Fields was the one...if that was even his name.

All right. Get the rest of your clothes on and get to the stable.

Jared shoveled the last load of manure into the wheelbarrow and wiped his brow with his forearm. The physical labor of mucking out the stable had warmed his muscles. All he had left to do was spread fresh straw in the stalls. The horses were restless and in need of exercise, but at least they had grain and water. The cow hadn't been milked yet and was beginning to complain. Where was Talia? Maybe she decided to stay inside after all and cook breakfast.

The door opened. "'Bout time your majesty showed up," he teased. "Bossie over there has been complaining."

"Sorry. The stove didn't want to light this morning." She smiled up, shyly fluttering her dark lashes. "Besides her name is Daisy, not Bossie."

"I stand corrected." He stretched his shoulders. "I'll dump the wheelbarrow around back and pick up more wood while I'm at it."

Talia nodded, and without another word, she grabbed the milking stool and bucket, then set about relieving the cow's distress.

He watched until he heard the milk spurting against the metal bucket, then picked up the barrow's handles and started rolling it outside.

The air was still brisk and thankfully fresh after the close confines of the stable. Talia seemed reserved. Still put out by about his snooping around, no doubt. If she didn't get over it, matters between them could grow uncomfortable. He needed her trust if he was going to root out the truth of Montrose's death. His superior at the agency was anxious to wrap up the case.

Around back, he dumped the manure and picked up a load of firewood. As he was heading back to the front of the stable, he heard a crack, looked up and dodged. A long shard of ice fell, barely missing his shoulder.

Whew! Close call. But on the good side, if ice was starting to fall, the temperature must be warming up.

He met a frowning Talia at the stable door. "I hate to discard all the fresh milk, but it's more than we can use," she said.

"I'll take care of it." He held out his hand for the bucket.

"I still have to throw down fresh straw in the stalls."

She responded with a quick nod. "I'll start breakfast, then."

Jared watched her trudge back to the ranch house. Even bundled with heavy clothing and hampered by snow, her natural grace was evident. Something about her manner worried him. And the edge to her voice. Businesslike but with an underlying current of...what—anger?

Yes. Had to be anger. His careless snooping. Couldn't undo it. He'd have to seduce her out of her bad mood. He smiled at the thought of bedding her again. Given the weather conditions, what else was there to occupy their time?

His stomach growled, reminding him it was time to finish his morning chores and get back inside. Spreading fresh straw around the stalls, he spoke softly to the two horses. Talia's dappled mare was a gentle creature and not nearly as restless as Midnight. "Sorry, fella. You wouldn't like it out there. Maybe the snow will end soon." The stallion nickered and tossed his head as if he actually understood.

"Okay, Daisy, here's some fresh straw." Standing between the milk cow and the rear stable wall, he shook an armful of straw onto the floor. He bent over to even it out a bit, when he heard another cracking sound. More ice falling from the stable roof.

But, startled by the unexpected noise, the cow bellowed and whipped her hindquarters into Jared, knocking him off his feet and into the wall. He crashed to the floor. Gingerly testing his limbs, he found he had a bruised hip but was otherwise okay. "Easy girl. Easy," he said, intending to get to his feet and out of her way.

But fate—the bitch—had something else in mind.

Before he could scramble to his feet, the cow backed up and stepped on his lower leg, a grazing step, yet a stunning burst of pain shot through his leg as at least one bone splintered. He groaned and nearly passed out. Damned cow had broken his damned leg!

Holy fucking shit! Now the bitch of a cow was going to trample him to death before he could crawl out of her way. Using his forearms and his one good leg, he scooted as fast as he could out of range of her hindquarters and hooves.

He'd crawled only a few feet when the pain forced him to stop. Gasping from the agony of a broken bone, he waited until the pain eased a fraction. He inched into a sitting position with his back against a post, then tried to take stock of his injury. He felt along his calf. Felt the swelling, especially along the outside. As far as he could tell, the big bone in the lower leg was intact. And thank God, the bone wasn't protruding through the skin. That could mean an amputation at the least...or a death sentence at the worst. Still, he'd heard something snap. Must've been the smaller bone. All the same, it hurt like hell.

Grimacing with the effort it took and cursing, he half crawled, half scooted to the door. Dust and straw from the floor tickled his nose. He sneezed.

The prospect of crawling another hundred yards through the snow didn't hold much appeal. He glanced around the stable. If he could fashion something into a makeshift crutch, he might be able to hobble back to the house under his own steam. Otherwise, how long would it take an angry Talia to realize something was wrong?

He scooted around until he faced one of the support beams. *Careful.* "God!" He'd forgotten his hip was bruised, and now it was already stiffening up. If he could get to his knees, he could get on his feet—well, one of them, anyway. A shovel would do for supporting his weak side.

Jared gritted his teeth and rolled to his belly. A groan ripped from his throat. Damned if he couldn't feel the ends of the broken bone rubbing together. No matter. He had to get back to the house.

Pushing up from his elbows, he scooted his good leg underneath his body. Now for the other.

Pain spiked through his leg to his hip. Damn. Damn. Damn. He clenched his jaw and gasped for air until the pain lessened. While holding on to the beam, he shifted his weight to his injured side. At least that knee was steady enough. Then he brought his uninjured leg forward until his foot was flat on the stable floor. He sucked in a deep breath and, bunching his thigh muscles, straightened his good leg, pulling his body to a standing position.

Clinging to the post, Jared groaned and waited until the pain lessened. Once it had, he wiped the sweat from his brow. His good leg trembled, but his balance began to steady. He reached for the shovel.

Now all he had to do was hop a hundred yards through the snow to the ranch house. There he'd find a relatively warm kitchen and food. And Talia.

Dear, sweet Talia, who, if she knew why he was here, would probably shoot him and put him out of his misery.

Chapter Eleven

Natalia broke four eggs, gathered before the storm, into a bowl and started to whip them with a fork. Scrambled eggs would make a hearty breakfast, along with fried bacon and bread toasted in the oven. Too bad she didn't have all the ingredients on hand for *huevos rancheros*. Sarita made the best tortillas and salsa around. While Natalia could cook, the few dishes were plain and simple ones because her friend and housekeeper cook had always been there. And she cooked so much better.

And now because of that bastard's arrival, Sarita had left them alone and probably perished in the snowstorm. Natalia's throat tightened, and her hands shook. What she wouldn't give to punish the bastard. Poison him. Now that would serve him right.

As quickly as the drastic solution entered her mind, it fled. If she hadn't poisoned old Reginald during the eight horrible years of their marriage, she wasn't about to harm the man who'd saved her life.

Still, for all his fine manners, he was dangerous. And up to no good if he thought he was going to pin Reginald's death on her.

Where was he, anyway? How long did it take to spread a little straw?

Natalia dumped the eggs into a hot iron skillet. They sizzled as they hit the bacon grease left behind. The aroma hit her nose, making her mouth water and her stomach growl. While the eggs cooked, she continued whipping them. Light and fluffy was how she liked them.

She glanced toward the door. Her patience was wearing thin. If he didn't hurry his deceitful bones, the eggs would be cold and not worth eating. Four eggs were four eggs they wouldn't have tomorrow or the next day—however long this blasted snow was going to last. The hens in the henhouse normally didn't lay much in the winter, and that was providing they didn't freeze to death in the meantime.

Fine. Let the bastard starve. She dumped the scrambled eggs into a clean bowl and set it on the stovetop. Wiping her hands on her apron, she walked over to the door and peered out.

There he was. Finally.

But something was wrong. He was hobbling, holding on to something for support.

Forgetting her anger and ignoring the cold, she opened the door and rushed outside. "Here. Put your arm around my shoulder. I'm steadier than a stupid shovel," she said, taking the shovel and casting it aside. "What happened?" She wrapped her arm around his waist, providing additional support.

He gazed at her as if she were an oasis in the desert. "Let's just say your cow didn't care to be startled and lashed out—without true provocation, I might add."

The weight of his body was heavy, but together they

struggled back to the ranch house. "What did you do to the poor thing? Is Daisy all right?"

He stopped and stared. "Is *she* all right? She broke my damned leg."

"Can't be broken. You're putting weight on it."

"I heard it snap. Must be the smaller of the two bones. If the larger bone isn't broken, it can support weight, but it hurts like hell."

"I see. So *now* you're a doctor and obviously an expert in anatomy."

"Common sense. Besides, my older brother had a similar injury when he was a lad."

"Who stepped on him? Or should I say what?"

Jared grinned somewhat sheepishly. "Something fell on him."

"What?"

"Me."

"Figures." Natalia reached for the door and opened it. "Go on. Breakfast is getting cold."

"Talia, you're a heartless creature." He took his arm from around her shoulder.

"Heart*less*?" *Calm down. Don't give yourself away.* "I cooked breakfast, and I rescued you, for pity's sake. Hardly the actions of a *heartless* creature."

"Rescued? Hmph." He wrinkled his nose and sneered. "Hardly a rescue. I could've made it to the house."

"Yes, you could've. But don't deny you were glad to see me."

"I won't." He hobbled the rest of the way into the kitchen.

"Now sit. I hate cold eggs." Try as she might, she

couldn't keep the brusque tone from her voice.

Jared eased down onto one of the chairs. "Wait a minute." She pulled out another chair. "Prop your leg on this one." She reached for his boot and started to tug it off.

"Easy, woman. It's broken."

Natalia let out an exasperated sigh. "I'll be as easy as I can, but that boot has to come off before there's more swelling." Straddling his outstretched leg, she gently pulled off his boot, then removed the other with a great deal less moaning on Jared's part. "Now as soon as you eat, those pants are coming off. I'll pack some snow around the break. It'll help the swelling."

"Now who's acting like the doctor?" He pulled off his gloves and set them on the chair beside his outstretched foot.

"We've tended broken bones on this ranch before." At least Sarita had. Trying to hide her trepidation, Natalia stood with her hands on her hips. "You're not the first."

"I appreciate your expertise, then. Thank you, Talia."

If only she'd had expertise beyond watching Sarita's ministrations.

Even though the temptation to poison him, or at the very least to smack his face, was strong, his soft tone reminded her how tender he was in bed. How he'd seen to her pleasure as well as his own. Giving herself permission to smile, she said, "You're welcome. I guess it's the least I can do for the man who saved my life." Even if that same man was trying to find proof she'd had her husband murdered.

She set the bowl of eggs on the table, along with a platter of bacon and buttered toast. "I trust you can help yourself. Nothing wrong with your hands?" She softened her words with another smile to keep from gritting her teeth.

Easy. Easy. He was bound to get suspicious with the way she was acting.

Jared held up his hands and wiggled his fingers. "All present and accounted for, ma'am."

"I'll get a jar of preserves from the pantry. Just be a minute." She fled the kitchen for the sanctuary of the storeroom. Her hands started shaking again. She felt like her whole body was about to explode. Somehow she must regain a modicum of self-control. After several deep breaths, she felt calmer. At least calm enough to face him without taking an iron skillet to his head.

Snatching a jar of gooseberry preserves from the shelf, she took one more breath, then headed back to the kitchen and Jared.

Despite the throbbing in his leg, Jared wasn't about to let Talia's delicious breakfast go to waste. He ate a couple of bites of his eggs and then crunched down on a piece of bacon. He let out a moan of satisfaction. Eggs were still warm and the bacon was crisp, the way he liked it. As hungry as he was, though, it would take a side of beef to fill him up.

Talia returned, bearing a jar of something. "Gooseberry preserves," she said. "Hope you like them."

Her tone of voice clearly said she hoped he'd choke. Obviously, his untimely snooping still angered her. "Thank you. I'm sure it's delicious."

"Don't worry. I didn't make it. Sarita did. I'm afraid I've been overly dependent on her." A frown pulled her dark, wing-like brows together. "I can't imagine what it will be like to live here without her." Her bottom lip trembled. "She was the one who kept me going through eight years of hell."

He reached across and stroked the back of her hand. "I'm sure she made it home in time. You'll see." More words of false hope, but hope was all he had to offer.

"I hope you're right." She reached for a piece of toast and spread a dab of preserves over it. She took one bite; then, like an jittery grasshopper, she sprang from her chair.

"What is it?"

"Your leg. I'll pack your leg with snow now. I don't want to wait. There's some oilcloth stored in the pantry I can use."

"Please. Sit down and eat. My let's not hurting...as long as I don't move." Not close to the truth. It throbbed and ached like it was caught in a vise. But Talia needed to eat and keep up her strength.

"Are you sure?" she asked, hesitating.

"I'm sure."

Talia picked up a strip of bacon and used it to point at him. "I hope you realize you're not going back outside. *I'll* feed the horses and do the rest of the morning chores."

"No, you won't."

Damn. "I can manage with something like a cane. Or maybe I can fashion a crutch from something I find in the stable."

She shook her head. "Not necessary. Reginald had several canes. He thought they made him look important."

She rolled her eyes, then continued, "One of them should help you, at least move around in the house."

He chewed on a second piece of bacon. No point in arguing when her mood was volatile. Sitting around like an invalid while she did a man's work wasn't in his nature. Damn it. He'd taken her husband's clothes. Taken his place at the head of the table. Not the least of all, taken his place in Talia's bed. And none of it planned.

Without warning, the muscles in his injured leg spasmed, causing him to start and grimace with pain.

"What?" She jumped up. "You *are* in pain. I shouldn't have let you stop me—"

"Just a muscle spasm. Relax. It's over." Almost.

"How did they treat your brother's broken leg?"

Jared frowned. "He lay around for a couple of days with his leg elevated on pillows, an ice pack and a compression bandage."

"I knew it. As soon as you finish eating, you're going to bed, and you're going to allow me to take care of you. You wouldn't have been injured if not for helping me."

"You'll be sorry. I'm not as good a patient was my brother was." Another lie. His brother Garth had been a real bastard when he'd been injured. Jared had been his brother's servant for the duration of his injury, and his brother had taken full advantage. *"More ice. Move my leg. Rewrap the bandage. Get my crutch."*

"I don't expect you to be a good patient. But I do expect you to follow my orders to the letter."

"That remains to be seen. I'm no good at following orders, not even those of someone as beautiful as you."

A quick smile flashed across her face, but there

remained a cloud of anger hovering in her expression. Couldn't blame her. Here she was in a freakish snowstorm, saddled with an invalid. He'd be put out too.

"Pretty words won't keep me from restraining you in bed."

"Restraints?" The image of being tied to her bed made him think of tying *her* down and making love all night. But for now that particular activity would have to wait.

"What's so amusing?"

"Nothing. Just a random thought."

A spark of humor lit her eyes, and a half smile lifted one corner of her mouth, showing her dimple. "You're in no shape to be having random thoughts at all, especially those."

"No need to remind me."

"Good. Are you finished?" She glanced at his empty plate. "Do you want more?"

"There's a lot I want."

"To eat," she said with steel in her voice.

"No, ma'am. I've had enough."

"Then to bed with you. I don't believe you are so arrogant as to believe you can do without medical care. You could lose your leg."

"I'm not going to lose my damned leg."

"*Señor* Fields, your language—"

"Talia, we are so far beyond quibbling over my language."

"We are not in the bedroom, sir." She drew her body into a rigid stance, her nose in the air. "I won't stand for bad language, neither in my drawing room nor in my kitchen."

"You have any idea how beautiful you are when you get all huffy?"

"Enough! Off to bed." She stood with her hands on her hips. "I'll tear sheets to bandage your leg, and then I'll pack it with snow. Or *maybe* I should locate a saw and remedy the situation entirely."

"A saw?" He shoved his plate away and stood on his good foot. "Where's that cane, or will you let me put my arm around you again?"

"I'll fetch a cane." She paused. "But if you feel you need additional support, I'd be a poor hostess to refuse assistance."

"Great. Now you've gone from being a delightful woman to an uptight society dame. In case you're interested, I'd prefer Talia to the stuffy Mrs. Montrose. Please, ma'am. May Talia come out and play?"

She let out an exasperated huff and fled the kitchen.

Whatever had gotten Talia's knickers in a twist? Perhaps his brief inspection of her financial ledgers had upset her more than she'd let on. Maybe she *was* hiding something. But what? More than likely that was the true reason for her underlying irritation than any inconvenience his accident caused.

Talia returned quickly, brandishing a black cane topped with a gold serpent's head. "Here. This one should suit you quite well," she said with a fixed smile and eyes as black as the cane's ebony wood.

Thankful she didn't hit him over the head with it, he accepted the cane with a polite nod. Might as well address the situation now. "Talia, I'm sorry."

She shot him a calculating glance. "Whatever do you

have to be sorry about?"

"For invading your privacy this morning. I know you're still angry. And for my clumsiness. As soon as the weather abates, I promise I'll get out of your hair."

He shifted the cane to his left hand and took a step. Pain shot from his right calf to his knee. He gasped. "Damn."

Talia rushed to his side. "Hold on to me."

He shook his head and brushed her away. "I can make it, now that I know what to expect." Carefully, he took another step. The pain was the same, but he clenched his teeth and continued in his halting fashion.

Somewhere behind him, Talia was muttering, "Stubborn ass."

Glad she couldn't see his face, he smiled. "Mrs. Montrose—your language."

"If you weren't already injured, I'd kick you."

"Then I shall be ever grateful for your cow's excitable nature."

Another huff. She sped around him and opened the door to *her* bedchamber. All was not lost.

As if she'd read his mind, she said, "Don't think just because you'll be in my bedroom that anything is going to happen. It'll just be easier to care for you if we're in the same—"

"I understand completely and appreciate your concern." He almost said, *my lady.* Likely that would've angered her further.

"After you're settled, I'll add some wood to the fire," she said. She scurried over to the far side of the bed and began straightening the linens in quick, jerky movements. "Would you prefer the bed or maybe the chaise for now?"

"The chaise." He hobbled over to the chair and stretched out, unable to keep from groaning.

Wrinkling her nose, she leaned over his foot and propped it on pillows she took from the bed. "You need to come out of those clothes. I must see to your leg. Besides, they smell of manure."

"You'd smell of manure too, if you'd had to crawl—"

"No doubt," she said with a slight smile, cutting off his litany of excuses.

"If you'll leave me something to change into, I can get these off. You can go on and do whatever you need to do." He waved her away. Last thing he needed was her hovering over him like he was an infant. "Just go on."

"Call me."

He waited until she closed the door to remove his shirt. Talia was right. It was overripe with manure and sweat. What he wouldn't give for a hot bath. He unbuckled his belt, then unbuttoned the denim trousers. Working them down over his butt was no easy feat, but he managed. He extricated his good leg, then, groaning, he worked the trousers down over his bad leg using his left foot.

He gasped with relief when the denim trousers hit the floor. Mouth dry, he swallowed, then glanced at his right leg. His calf was bruised and swollen, more on the outer aspect than the inner. Carefully, he touched the area and winced. Thankfully, the heavy creature's hoof had stepped on him with more of a glancing blow than a direct step.

Even so, it throbbed like a son of a bitch. No doubt about it. In spite of the pain, his biggest regret was that the injury would hamper his investigation.

*

Natalia hesitated a moment and set two logs on the floor beside her. Trying not to think about the ordeals to come, she tapped on the door, then opened it. Jared was bare from the waist up. Again, she couldn't help but admire his lean-muscled body and remember how he'd felt under her touch. *Dios.* She shook her head. How he looked and felt weren't important. At least he'd managed to rid himself of his smelly outer garments. All things considered, she probably didn't smell much better, but at least she hadn't crawled around on the stable floor.

She picked up the logs and carried them inside. Kneeling by the fire, she added one of the logs and said, "We'll keep the fire going in this room to keep you from getting chilled." She got to her feet, picked up his discarded clothing and, holding them away from her body, took them from the room. Not having any way to wash them, she'd just toss them out the back door and dispose of them the next time she went out to the stable.

She gathered up the strips of linen she'd torn while he undressed and carried them back to her bedroom.

His expression brightened when she entered the room, and made her heart beat faster. Hold on. Under no circumstances would she let him affect her so. The man was a Pinkerton agent and here to ruin her life.

But for now, there was his injury to deal with. "All right, let me see what you've done."

"Pretty much what I thought—the small bone is the one broken. Got off lucky."

She nodded, taking in the discoloration and swelling.

"*Sí*, it could have been much worse."

"I'll take it easy today," he said, shrugging his wide, muscular shoulders. "But my brother was up and around in a couple of days, or he would've been if he hadn't decided to make my life a living hell."

"Well, you *did* break his leg."

"I did at that," he said with a wry, almost boyish smile.

Tilting her head to the side, she gazed down at his leg. "I guess I'd better wrap your leg now."

He nodded, his features contorted as if dreading the pain to come. "Make it tight. Start from the foot. Loop it around a couple of times in a figure eight."

She smiled, hesitating to admit her uncertainty. "I've never actually done this before. Sarita always took care of it. I wish I'd paid more attention."

"You can do it. I used to rewrap my brother's leg, and I was just a lad."

"That was very nice of you—"

"Yeah," he interrupted with a bark of laughter. "All things considered."

All right. If Jared could do it when a lad, then she, a mature woman, could as well. Chewing on her bottom lip, she looped one of the linen strips around his foot, then up around his ankle and back around his foot again.

"Once more," he said. "Make sure the end is caught by the second wrapping."

Nodding, she did as he suggested, then began wrapping upward from his ankle.

"Tighter."

She tugged on the linen, overlapping each edge with the next wrap. "Sorry. I know I'm hurting you."

Pale-faced, hands clenched, and gritting his teeth, Jared grew rigid the closer she came to his calf. "Just hurry up."

"You need to hold it up and support it while I get the linen around the back of your calf."

Jared raised his right leg, supporting it with both hands while she quickly wrapped the rest of his lower leg. "Tight enough?"

"Any tighter and you might as well cut it off." His face grew red, and his leg trembled with the effort of holding it up. "You know, a shot or two of whiskey wouldn't be taken amiss."

"Of course. Why didn't I think of that?" After securing the top of the linen wrap, she gently removed his hands, substituting her own, and carefully rested his leg back down on the pillows.

"I'll be right back."

In all honesty, it was difficult to remain angry when he was in so much pain and needed her so badly. Reginald had never needed her. No one had.

Chapter Twelve

Stranded by a freak snowstorm. Hampered by an untimely accident. Dependent on the good graces of the woman he was assigned to investigate. Not to mention mesmerized by the woman's beauty and passion. Was there a worse way to end his career as a Pinkerton? If there was, he couldn't imagine it.

Seemed like he'd hit a streak of bad luck. His last assignment in the Texas Hill Country resulted in the opposite of what he was ordered to achieve. The young woman he'd returned to her fiancé turned out to be anything but happy. Starlight Tyler had run away when her mother had brokered an engagement with Jared's client, who turned out to be a bona fide sadist. In the long run, Jared had decided to protect her from his client until her real love, the sheriff of a neighboring county, could mount a rescue. To his shame, it turned out Jared needed rescuing himself after the client's henchmen jumped him and locked him up. Starlight was fiery, beautiful and quite a handful, and Sheriff Cordero Tate was welcome to her.

Jared's superiors at Pinkerton weren't happy, but he couldn't have lived with himself if he'd just turned that young woman over to a man who was intent on abusing her for his own sick gratification. There were many operatives at the agency who followed orders to the letter. It was the job for which they were paid, and they did it. No matter what the job was. No matter who was hurt.

No doubt about it, a paycheck from Pinkerton's was money in the bank and more dependable than any stray gambling winnings he picked up along the way. Risking his career for the sake of yet another woman could well prove the end of steady employment. And that was no way to show gratitude to the friend who'd recommended him for the position.

This wasn't the life he'd planned. Hell, he hadn't planned anything beyond university. Being disowned during his third year had put a crimp in his social standing and any plans he might've made after completing his education.

Another muscle spasm cut short his reverie. Damn. Where was she? Where was that whiskey? "Talia!"

She returned with a rush, a pile of folded clothes over one arm and a bottle of whiskey in her other. "I thought you might like some clean clothes. I wish we could bathe. Maybe I can melt some snow so that we can at least sponge clean. As for your—uh, bodily needs—"

"My *needs*? Never you mind. I'll manage my needs." He straightened up, snatched the shirt and started redressing. The very idea of her mentioning his bodily needs, much less allowing her to attend to them, was too horrifying to contemplate.

Talia laughed. "I had no idea you were so modest, *Señor* Fields."

"If I couldn't—you know—manage, then I'd rather be dead." Indeed, he would drag his body to the necessary before he'd depend on Talia for such.

"I was going to say, before you so rudely interrupted me, that Reginald installed a water closet in one of the rooms we seldom used. It's the door next to his bedchamber." She sat on the edge of the chaise and handed him a bottle of whiskey. "Here," she said in a soothing voice. "Perhaps, this will ease your pain somewhat and temper your mood."

"Nothing wrong with my mood." He held the bottle to his lips and gulped down what turned out to be a very fine Scotch whiskey. "Nothing wrong with your late husband's taste in liquor either."

"Only the very best would do for dear departed Reginald Montrose. Most of all, *I* was never good enough." As she leaned forward, her eyes glimmering, she smiled and said, "I'll risk your thinking ill of me, but I had him buried in the cheapest pine box available. Food for worms, guaranteed."

Jared reared back, rubbing his chin. "Jesus, Talia! You have a vengeful streak."

"'Tis true. And you would do well to remember it." Tweaking his nose, she rose from the chaise. She headed toward the door, her rounded hips swaying, then stopped and over her shoulder said with her most innocent smile, "I'll be getting that snowpack now."

In spite of his surprise at Talia's bold-as-brass statement, he couldn't help but admire the passion of her underlying threat. No doubt Montrose got exactly what he deserved. However, Jared, not Montrose, was now the man caught in her clutches, so to speak. Still, he wasn't afraid. In spite of her take-no-prisoners, frank speech, she possessed a good heart.

It went without saying the elder Montrose wouldn't take Jared's personal assessment as proof of anything. The only thing he could do, if the damned snow ever melted, was find out who else might've wanted Montrose dead. If the man was as arrogant and despised as reported, he must've made more enemies than just his wife.

The door to the bedroom opened, and Talia entered carrying what was apparently an oilcloth full of snow. She spread a bath towel over his lower leg, then set the cold pack on top of the towel.

He tensed from the shock of the snow pack. "Cold," he said with a mock shiver and took another gulp of whiskey. The smooth liquor warmed as it slid down his throat. Damned good stuff.

She shot him a quick smile. "That's the point. I found some ice that slid off the roof and broke it up. It won't melt as quickly as the snow."

"Thank you." This woman was *not* a killer. Might as well get it over with. Had to question her about her husband's death. Frowning, he leaned forward. "Talia, what do you think? Was your husband intentionally murdered?"

"He is dead," she said, matter-of-fact. "I would say the answer to that is a resounding '*Sí*'."

"There's a difference between a bar fight that goes too far and a death that's ordered and carried out."

Twisting her hair off her neck, she shrugged. "I confess I never thought too much about it." Not meeting his gaze, she stared over his shoulder. "I was too relieved he was out of my life."

"But as his wife, you had the greatest motive. Or did he

have enemies—other than you? Did Sheriff Moulton question you at all?" Best find out what he could before he slipped into the whiskey's warm embrace.

A clear expression of calculation passed across her face, but it was fleeting. "No. He merely came here and informed me Reginald was dead. That he'd been killed in a bar fight. I'd been at the ranch all day and all evening. Sarita was here with me, as well as Reginald's fancy cook from back East. He may have questioned the servants regarding how we got along, but he never questioned me directly."

"How did you learn the truth about your husband's death?"

"*Sí*, the truth." She shot him a rueful smile. "The very next day. Bad news travels fast in a small town, and a scandal spreads like wildfire. Needless to say, every woman who called on me—some of them for the first time ever—fed me the sordid details. So very apologetic. So very sympathetic, and *so* delighted to spread the filthy tale they nearly vibrated with it."

"I'm sorry, Talia. It must've been rough."

"After the third busybody, I quit receiving callers." Avoiding his gaze, she stared at her hands folded in her lap. Then just as suddenly, she looked at him, her dark eyes piercing. "Who *are* you, Jared? Is that even your name?"

Damn. He'd gone too far. Asked too many leading questions. But he wasn't ready to reveal his identity. Not yet.

He shrugged. "The puzzle of it intrigues me."

"If I didn't know better..." She paused, challenging him with her eyes. "I would think you're questioning me as if you were a lawyer...or something."

Or something? Suspicion was unmistakable in her skeptical expression. "Anyone would have questions about your husband's death." Still, he hated questioning the woman he'd made love to only last night. As much as he wanted to reveal his identity, he couldn't risk it.

Her regal nose went up in the air. "*I* don't. I simply thank the Blessed Mother for her intervention."

"Convenient that it worked out that way." He couldn't keep the biting tone from his words, no matter how hard he tried. "What if it hadn't? Would you have lived the rest of your life imprisoned by a miserable marriage?"

"What other choice did I have?" Her dark eyes widened. "Marriage is for life."

The sincerity when she said "*for life*" got to him. "You could've paid someone to kill him."

"I know what you think. And *who* you are. Jared Fields, Pinkerton agent!"

She knows! How? When? He took a hurried swallow of the mellow scotch.

"While you were outside injuring yourself, I did some snooping of my own. Very careless of you to leave that telegram in your pocket. I didn't kill my husband, and I didn't order anyone else to do it either!"

She rose, her fists clenched at her sides and fire in her eyes. If he didn't know her as well as he did, she appeared as if she might just want to kill Jared instead.

He began, "I wanted to tell you—"

"Like hell you did." She folded her arms across her chest. "You've had plenty of time to tell me what a low-down skunk you are. Like when we were in bed. Like when I found you going through my ledgers. I should break your other leg. Who hired you, Pinkerton?" She paced up and down the room, waving her hands in the air. "Tell me! I know it was Reginald's father, wasn't it? Reginald received a letter from him every year, telling him to get rid of his Mexican whore. I—who have the finest blood of the Spanish conquistadores flowing through my veins."

He could well believe it. She was all righteous indignation and regal beauty rolled into one package. "All right. I'll tell you everything. First, I don't believe you had your husband killed. Second, if you were going to kill him, it would be in a fit of anger, not by hiring someone to do it." Although she seemed to be in near-murderous pique right now, Jared thought, hugging the bottle. "Yes, it was your father-in-law who hired the Pinkerton Agency. I am one of their agents, and I was sent here to investigate your husband's death. To see if you had anything to do with it. And if you did, I was to bring you to justice."

"And if not...?"

"If not, then I was to bring you back to New York City—"

"New York City? Why would his father want the Mexican whore brought there?"

"In case there was an heir involved."

"An heir?" she scoffed. "No. He just wanted to regain control of whatever money Reginald hadn't gambled away. You know, there's no real money left. He found gold but gave it to my father for the land and cattle. My father drove a *very* hard bargain. And now, that's all there is—the land and the cattle. But I know how to run a cattle ranch. We are self-sufficient, depending on..." A cloud crossed her face.

"What is it?"

"The cattle were in La Mesa," she said, "waiting for the

train to take them to market. If they didn't get loaded before the snowstorm hit, I could lose them all."

Her stricken expression touched him. He cared more about Talia losing her cattle than he could've ever imagined. He rushed to encourage her. "Maybe it won't be as bad in town. They're not marooned there like we are here."

"It could be just as bad. What if the train was delayed by the snow in the mountains?" She sank onto the chaise beside him, covering her face with her hands. "What will I do? If the cattle don't make it to market, I'll lose the money they would have brought. If I lose the cattle, I could lose the land. And I *can't* lose the land. I've put up with too much. Suffered the pain and humiliation of being Reginald's Mexican slut. The one he didn't want...except to use. Certainly not a woman he'd father a child with."

Jared set the whiskey bottle aside, then cradled her in his arms, inhaling her womanly scent. How had she managed to stay so fresh when he hadn't? Another question: What if *he'd* already fathered a child with Talia? How could he just leave her with a failing ranch if there was a child on the way? *His* child. If there was, it was too soon to know. "It'll work out. You'll see." More useless words of hope.

"Don't patronize me, Pinkerton." Sniffing, Talia squirmed free of his embrace. "I know it'll work out. I'm strong. I can take anything fortune sends my way. I always have."

"I don't doubt it. What if I stay on after the snow melts?" The words were out of his mouth like runaway horses before he could rein them in. What in blue blazes was he saying?

"Stay on? Why would you do that?"

"What if we've made a child, Talia?"

"A child?" Realization dawned in her eyes. They lit as from within; then she shuttered them and averted her gaze. "I can raise a child on my own."

"A child should have a father to love him as well as a mother. My father—"

"*Mine* never loved me," she said, her dark gaze flashing. "Or if he did, he had a miserable way of demonstrating it. No. I'll not have another man ruling my life. Not even one as handsome as you, *Pinkerton*."

Every time she uttered the word Pinkerton, it sounded more and more like a curse. "What would the townsfolk think, or worse, say?"

"They wouldn't have to know. If I'm already with child, I'll say it was Reginald's."

"And then Reginald's father—"

She flipped her hair over her shoulder. "To hell with his father. Short of his coming here and dragging me to New York, there's nothing he can do."

"That's what *I've* been paid to do, Talia," he said, gently reminding her of his mission.

"But you're not going to, are you?" She gazed up at him, her expression soft but full of shadows. "No, I can see into your heart. You're a good man, Pinkerton, in spite of what you've been hired to do."

Her trust in his innate goodness touched him in a place he'd guarded and long thought dead—his heart. This woman unlocked feelings he'd never before experienced, much less acknowledged. She was tough on the outside and yet so soft beneath. More than anything, he wanted to protect her from everything and everyone.

"No. I won't make you do anything you don't want to." Was this feeling what his university friends called "falling in love"? Was it caring more about her life than his? Was it putting her interests ahead of his?

"What's wrong? Why are you looking at me like that?"

"Like how?"

"I don't know how." Her winged brows drew together in a frown. "You're confusing me. You've gone soft."

"I assure you, in spite of my injury, that's not the case." Indeed, his cock was painfully hard, and if he could just manage to bury it deep inside her hot, wet pussy, he would. Broken leg be damned.

He took her hand and placed it on his crotch. "Feel for yourself."

She rubbed his cock through his undergarments. "Truthfulness is a good thing in a man," she said with a wry grin. "And in the face of adversity, a hard cock is even better."

Emotion swelled, almost choking him. Talia was a marvel of a woman who ran the gamut of emotions from enraged to girlish to passionate beyond any man's imaginings. He swallowed hard. "Perhaps we could..."

"Aren't you supposed to be in pain?" she asked him straightway.

He couldn't help but grin. No bullshitting around with this woman. The words he'd never uttered to any woman were right there on his lips. Could he actually say them? Come this close to risking everything. Maybe the whiskey had made his mind reckless. Could Talia really overlook all his lies?

"You need to be in bed, all right. Alone." For all her passion, she sounded like a strict schoolteacher reprimanding a misbehaving student.

"Talia, I love you." The words came out softly, but never had he meant any statement so earnestly. Lies came easily to a Pinkerton agent. He'd lied often and well, but telling Talia he loved her gave his heart a lift and a freedom he'd never known.

Her gaze widened as if she'd seen or heard something horrible. "No!" Clasping her hand over her mouth, she sprang from her spot on the chaise and ran from the room.

Fuck. Now what had he done wrong?

At least she hadn't taken the whiskey with her. He reached for the bottle.

Chapter Thirteen

With Jared's simple declaration of love ringing in her ears, Natalia fled to the kitchen, the one place in the entire house she associated with comfort and warmth. No man had ever told her he loved her. To her father, she'd been an irritation, a constant reminder of the son and heir he didn't have. At best, she was a commodity for barter. Her husband—hah, to him she was the unwelcome remnant of a business transaction, the Mexican *putana*.

Gasping for air and shaking from fear, she sobbed into a towel. Why *now* did this Pinkerton proclaim his love so quietly and sincerely? So unexpectedly?

Was it part of his underhanded plan to make her confess to playing a part in Reginald's death? As much as she hated her dead husband, and as much as she hoped he burned in hell for the way he treated her, she'd played no part in his death.

Dios. No matter how she wanted to believe and needed to believe, how could she trust the Pinkerton? How could she trust any man with her inheritance, her future, or her heart?

Try as she might, she couldn't erase the thoughts of

spending the rest of her life with him, working together to run the ranch, even having his children...being a real family. Even if he loved her now, would he stick around? Jared was a man whose eyes were always fixed on the next horizon. Could he be satisfied with the life of a rancher?

She sniffed and dried her eyes. Time to stop caterwauling like a child. No matter what he said or promised, they were marooned in the worst snowstorm she'd ever experienced. Plenty of time enough to find answers to all her questions.

Distance. Keeping busy and keeping her distance would give her time to reflect. Why should she worry? Men would say anything to get what they wanted. More than likely the Pinkerton was already sorry he'd said he loved her, or was it just the whiskey talking? In time, they could go back to the way they were before—wary adversaries.

So, what now? The answer was simple: clean up the kitchen.

After clearing the table, she scraped the dishes and set them aside, then tried pumping the handle to the water pump. No water. She let out a heavy sigh. The dishes would just have to wait until the pipe that ran from the well to the house thawed. Heaven only knew when it would. So much for Reginald's insistence on modern conveniences.

Then dinner, or lunch, as Reginald deemed the midday meal. There were vegetables in the root cellar and smoked hams hanging from the beams.

Sí, she would have plenty to do preparing the next meal.

"Talia. Talk to me."

Startled to hear Jared's throaty voice so near, she whirled and discovered him leaning against the arched doorway. "What are you doing? You should be lying down with your leg propped on a pillow."

"Why are you upset? Only said what I felt."

Folding her arms across her breasts, she took a step backward. "I don't trust your words. Or your feelings. I don't trust *you*."

"I saved your life. That oughta be worth something. You jus' 'bout saved mine." His words were slurred, and to her horror, his body began to weave.

Without a second thought, she ran to him and grabbed him around the waist. "Just lean on me. And back to bed you go, so you can sleep this off."

"Don't wanna go back to bed. Talia, I love you."

"Never fails," she muttered. "Get a man drunk and all of a sudden he's madly in love. Anyone would do. That's all I am to you, Pinkerton, a warm body and a nursemaid."

He leaned heavily against her and mumbled, "Not sho. I loved you from the firs' time I saw you. Honesh."

"What did you do? Drink the rest of the bottle?"

"It was ver' fine shtuff. Makes my leg feel sho mush betta."

Guiding him down the central hallway, she wrinkled her nose and averted her face from his liquored breath. "What if that was the only bottle of whiskey I had? Then what would you do to ease the pain?"

"Make love." He smiled, a ridiculous, rather lopsided but endearing grin that warmed her heart. "That'll make ever'thing go 'way."

"Make love? You're hopeless, as well as drunk."

"Don' say that. I love you."

He was leaning on her, his body getting heavier by the

moment. "Almost there," she said, maneuvering him through the doorway.

"Wanna go to bed with you. Leg doeshn't hurt now. Let's make babies, Talia. I wanna have your babies."

Caramba, the man was *loco*. "Considering your current state of inebriation, I doubt you'd be up to the task."

"But if I was..." Together they stumbled to the chaise. He flopped with a groan. "My leg hurts."

She bent over and eased his injured leg onto the chaise. She covered him with a counterpane from the bed. "Sleep it off, Pinkerton," she said softly. "We'll discuss it later." By then he would have forgotten about making love or babies. If only she could have met him years ago...before Reginald swooped into La Mesa and dazzled her father with the lure of newfound gold.

Sighing, she replaced the ice pack on his leg. Making love with Jared was everything she'd ever hoped it would be. Having his children, working the ranch and cattle together—those were dreams that could never be. She'd suffered too much to risk everything for the love of any man, especially a man who might grow restless and leave her alone without a second thought.

Jared tugged on the coverlet and allowed the warmth from the fire and the whiskey heat in his belly to draw him into uneasy slumber. Visions of a raven swooped and swirled in a moonlit night sky; then the bird alighted on his shoulder with needle-sharp talons sinking into his body. When he turned to brush the bird away, he came face-to-face with a raven-haired beauty with ebon eyes that flashed with fire.

Unable to move, he stood mired to the spot, rooted as surely as if he'd sprouted and grown there. The woman danced around him, always out of reach, taunting him with her body, offering him kisses, then darting away. He wanted her more than he'd wanted any other woman. Had to have her.

But her high-pitched laughter cut through him. He could never have her, the laughter seemed to say. He wasn't good enough for her or rich enough. He would never amount to anything. Worthless. An embarrassment to the family. The voice deepened. His father.

The woman flew away, replaced by a tall, forbidding bear who laughed. Bitter, derisive and harsh.

That was his old man to a T.

Rage rushed through Jared, setting his body aflame. *Try to run. Escape. No use.* A thick vine wrapped around his leg and held him fast. And still as the flames licked his body and his body quivered, he heard his father's laughter...and the faint echoing call of the raven.

"Talia! Don't leave me."

Surely they wouldn't be marooned that long. The ever-present wind had died down. Maybe it was her imagination, but it seemed like it might've quit snowing quite so hard.

There were plenty of dried beans, cornmeal and flour. Poor Jared. His meals would've been a lot better if Sarita had stayed. Likely she would have been better off too. Blessed Mother protect her.

All right. The inventory more or less complete, she picked up what she needed to prepare their midday meal. They would have the leftovers for supper.

She set the goods on the table, almost dropping them at the sound of a hoarse yell.

Jared.

She heaved a sigh. Now what? She'd hoped to get their next meal started before having to deal with him again. He might be a wonderful lover, but he was a terrible patient. Typical of his sex.

She wiped her hands on her apron. "Coming."

When she entered her bedroom, she found him shaking with a hard chill. She reached to touch his forehead. Burning hot. His eyes were glazed with fever.

"I'm so..." Jared grabbed her hand. "Don't go. I'll be a good boy. I promise, Father. I promise."

She pulled another counterpane from her bed and started to cover him. No. That didn't make sense. Somehow, she had to cool him down. The ice pack. She pulled it from his leg and placed it on his chest. More. She needed more ice.

"It's cold." He tugged on the ice pack and threw it to the floor.

"Stop it." She retrieved the pack and replaced it. "You've a fever. The ice will help break it."

"I'm so cold." His plaintive tone was that of a child who didn't understand why he was being mistreated.

She rushed from the room to find another oilcloth to fill with snow and ice.

***

*

Outside, the cold was still bitter, but the wind was a mere breeze compared to what it had been the day and night before. Without the fierce wind blowing the snow, she could even make out the stables in the distance. That was a definite improvement, even though she couldn't make out the mountain ridge that rimmed the western edge of the ranch. Maybe there *would* be a thaw before spring. After all, she remembered a couple of Novembers which were unseasonably warm. Hurriedly, she filled snow and ice into two oilcloth packs, a small one for his head and the larger one for his body.

She had to get back. Poor Jared was out of his head. And no telling what he might do without her there to corral him.

Back inside, she rushed to her bedroom with the packs and found him attempting to get off the chaise. As weak as a newborn foal, he struggled with an unseen foe.

She sped to his side and restrained him. "Stop it!"

"Go 'way. Make him stop. He's hurting me."

Again his tone was that of a child's, not the grown man she knew. What childhood nightmares were troubling his rest, she could only imagine. "It's all right. I won't let anyone hurt you. But you have to let me cool you down, Jared." She smoothed the hair from his forehead. So very hot. "It's for your own good. Please let me."

"Okay, Mama. Just make Father go 'way."

Dios, what had his father done to him? "He's gone now. Go back to sleep, darling. *Mami's* here." Sitting by him on the chaise, she cradled his head, tears trickling down her cheeks. "Poor *bebé*." No matter how her father had treated her like a nuisance, he'd never beaten her.

Jared quieted, though his body still shook with the chills of a rising fever. She eased from the chaise and picked up the smaller oilcloth pack, placing it on his forehead.

He shook his head. "No, Mama. Cold."

"It's all right, *bebé*. *Mami* loves you." Her throat closed with the realization her words were true. There, he had his answer, but he was too sick to know. She stroked his cheek. "It's for your own good. You know *Mami's* always right."

He nodded slowly.

Whether or not his agreeable nature would continue after she placed the larger pack on him, she'd soon know. Keeping one layer of clothing over his chest, she applied the snow pack. His body started in response to the chill. "Easy, *hijo*," she said in her most soothing voice.

He shook his head and tugged weakly on the pack. Gently taking his hands, she placed them by his sides. She glanced around the room. For his safety's sake, she'd have to stay with him until his fever broke or at least as long as he wasn't in his right mind.

What was it Sarita said? "*Alimenta un resfriado. Mata de hambre una fiebre.*" Feed a cold, starve a fever? He wouldn't be eating for a while, but he needed liquids. Whether or not she could get any down him was another matter entirely.

Think. Think. What else had Sarita done when Natalia had a fever? She'd been a very healthy child and could remember only one instance at thirteen when she was extremely ill. Other than keeping her cool and giving her liquids, there was a bitter-tasting tea Sarita had given her.

What was the name of it, and more importantly, was there any in Sarita's store of medicinal herbs?

Willow-bark tea? *Sí*. That was it. But should she leave Jared long enough to find the herb? She studied her charge. He'd quieted for the moment, although his body seemed to twitch now and then. At least he wasn't fighting or having nightmares.

She really didn't like seeing him twitch. Something wasn't right. She'd better find that damn herb and make the tea. Chewing her lip, she rushed from the room and ran to the storeroom. Sarita kept the woven basket of medicinal herbs on the topmost shelf. On tiptoe, Natalia pulled down the basket and located the herb. If she remembered Sarita's instructions correctly, a teaspoon of the powdered herb had to be soaked for eight hours in a cup of cold water, then strained. Hopefully, she could keep him comfortable with the ice-and-snow packs until the willow-bark tea was ready.

Sarita had made Natalia drink three cups of the bitter stuff a day for several days until her fever dissipated. She'd had given Natalia the instructions for the tea's preparation along with a supply of medicinal herbs on the occasion of her marriage. Apparently, every wife needed her own supply of herbs to treat her family's illnesses.

Too bad there hadn't been a cure for meanness of spirit included. She would've dosed Reginald with that one daily.

She brought in a soup pot full of snow and set it on the cookstove to melt. Once again she thanked the Blessed Mother that Sarita had been so thoughtful.

All right, back to check on her patient.

When she reentered the bedroom, Jared was lying

quietly on the chaise. She checked the ice packs; they'd need refilling soon. His forehead was still hot and his hands were trembling, but at least he wasn't having a hard chill.

Now back to the stove to see if the snow had started to melt. No point in getting the water warm, since the fever preparation had to steep in cold water. She brushed the hair back from her forehead and sighed. *Dios*, why did the damn stuff have to take so long to prepare? Maybe the ice-and-snow packs alone would be enough to break his fever.

Taking one last glance at Jared, she returned to the kitchen. She looked over the rim of the soup pot and gave the slush a stir. Enough of the snow had melted so she could prepare the first cup of the tea. Maybe steeping six hours would be sufficient. No, Sarita had given specific instructions. Eight hours.

She dipped into the slushy snow with the soup ladle and poured the cold water into a tin measuring cup, filling it half full, then another ladle to fill the cup. With care, she measured out a teaspoon of the precious herb, then said a quick prayer before dumping it into the cup. Giving the mixture a quick stir, she then left the mixture to steep.

The next few hours were a never-ending blur of changing out ice packs, which necessitated additional trips outside in the snow and coming back inside. Between that, sitting by his side to watch over him and tending the fire, she was numb with exhaustion. While the willow-bark tea steeped, she wiped his face over and over with cold, wet towels. She could only rouse him enough to get a few sips of water down. When he did rouse, he remained confused and still thought she was his mother. Since it seemed to calm him, Natalia continued with the pretense.

When she grew hungry to the point of feeling faint, she grabbed a piece of cornbread from the kitchen and nibbled on it while she watched over her charge.

She dragged a rocking chair from the drawing room into the bedroom. She didn't dare lie on the bed for fear she'd go to sleep. Even so, her eyelids grew heavy, but the striking of the long case clock in the hall brought her out of her doze. She counted the strokes.

Finally, the eight hours were up. She jumped from the rocker and rushed to grab the cup of tea. Damn stuff had better work, because Jared wasn't getting any better. What if he didn't get better? What if he died? She'd be all alone in this miserable snowstorm. What would be the point of going on without him?

Stop it. The isolation and not having anyone to rely on except herself was getting to her. The tea would bring Jared's fever down, and they would support each other until the storm was over, as they had before his fall.

When she entered the bedroom, he was in the throes of another chill. She flew to his side.

"Jared!"

His arms flailed about. She had to jump back to keep him from knocking the cup of herbal tea from her hand. She set the cup on a table out of his reach, then sat on the edge of the chaise. "Easy, *pequeño*, you need to calm down and drink the tea. It'll help you feel so much better. Be *mami*'s good boy."

"I'm always a good boy, Mama. Aren't I?"

"*Sí, bebé.* You are such a good boy. Now drink this tea for your *mami*."

"Yes, Mama," he said parting his parched lips to sip the liquid. "Ugh!" Shaking his head, he shut his eyes tightly and held his lips together. "Unh-uh," he mumbled, waving her away.

Damn it. He needed to drink the entire cup. "Jared, you must drink this for *mami*. You won't be my good boy if you don't."

"Aw-right." Keeping his eyes shut, he opened his mouth and hunched his shoulders in preparation for the bad taste.

This time, thankfully, he drank the rest of the cup. He finished the tea with a grimace, wiping his lips with the back of his hand. "Blech!"

Natalia wanted to laugh. He was so genuinely a little boy...a darling one at that. How wonderful it would be to have a small Jared to care for, to watch him grow from a baby to a grown man who would then have babies of his own. Maybe he was right. They might've already started a baby. With Sarita's help, she could raise the child...if her friend was still alive. *Please let her be all right. Please let this snow stop. And please let Jared's fever go down.*

She reclaimed the rocking chair and continued her watch. He'd already drifted into a light sleep, but his fingers still picked at the ice pack on his chest. Reaching over, she covered his strong, calloused hands with hers. Her touch always seemed to ease his suffering.

When he quieted, she leaned back in the rocker just to rest her eyes for a moment.

Jared awakened, rubbing the sleep from his eyes. What the hell? His hand went to his head and removed a makeshift ice pack. He dropped it to the floor, then pulled away a larger pack from his chest. Soaking wet, he shivered. The fire still burned, keeping the chill from the room.

Talia was asleep in a rocking chair, her beautiful face pale and drawn, her dark hair tousled and falling in waves about her shoulders.

"Talia..."

She shook herself awake and sat up straight. "What? I'm sorry I didn't mean to fall asleep. You're better," she said with a wide smile.

Grinning, he stretched his neck and shoulders. "Better than what?"

"Better than before. You were delirious."

"Sure I wasn't just drunk?" He wiped his mouth with his hand. "I'm pretty sure I finished off that bottle of whiskey."

"Oh, no. You were out of your head."

"Really? Damn." He yawned, then winced when the muscles in his leg cramped. "Leg's no better. And I'm soaking wet." He pulled at his union suit. "I'm kind of rank here. Sorry."

"I don't care how you smell. You're going to be all right." She leaned forward, reaching to touch his forehead. His hair was wet from sweat and the ice pack. "Thank the Blessed Mother, your fever has broken. I wasn't sure if the tea would work or not."

"The *tea*?"

"Willow-bark tea," she said, heaving a sigh. "I managed to get a cup down you...barely."

He swallowed. Damn if his tongue didn't feel like it was stuck to the roof of his mouth. "That accounts for the vile taste." He shook his head and gave a shiver.

"*Sí*. But you'll need several doses just to make sure your fever stays down."

He shut his eyes and grimaced. "Now that makes me wish I was still out of my head. Not looking forward to meeting that stuff again."

She smiled. A wonderful warm smile that gladdened his heart. In spite of her anger over learning his true identity and mission, she'd cared for him during the evening and night, getting little rest. Her ire and passion concealed the truly good human being inside, not to mention that her presence comforted him as no other woman's had.

"I hope you'll take it willingly this time," she said arching raven brows.

"I was difficult, was I?"

"Indeed. But you were a good *boy* after all. At least you were good for your *mami*."

"That's who I thought you were?"

"Most assuredly, Pinkerton. You were very sweet but made the most terrible face when it came time to drink the tea."

"Thank you," he said simply, his heart too full to say more. "I wouldn't have blamed you if you'd left me out in the snow to die."

Her dark eyes widened at his suggestion. "I admit I was tempted," she said with a casual shrug. "Should I have let you die in the snow after you rescued me from the same fate? I don't think so." She rose from the rocker. "Now let's get you into some dry clothes. The ice pack on your leg needs refreshing. You won't need the others as long as your fever stays down."

"Hold on. You need to get some sleep. If I'm not mistaken, you've been up most of the night. You kept the fire going, kept these icepacks filled and forced that bitter-tasting tea down me. You must be exhausted."

"It was nothing I wouldn't have done for anyone in a similar predicament." She shrugged as if his litany of her good deeds wasn't a big deal. "I might've dozed for a second here and there. I didn't mean to."

So he was nothing to her? Fine. "I'm awake. I'll get up and—"

"Pinkerton! You're not going anywhere. You need to stay off that leg another day at least. You need food...and a bath."

"Only if you take one with me." He grinned up at her and winked.

She rolled her eyes, and a hint of a smile twitched her full lips. "I'm afraid not. The copper tub isn't big enough for two."

"Wash my back?" he suggested hopefully.

"I think I could manage that sometime later." Talia set her hands on her hips. "For now, you'll have to settle for a sponge bath to prevent damage to your leg. You do remember you have a broken leg?"

He gritted his teeth. "Not likely to forget that." Glancing at the empty bottle on the floor, he put on his most charming grin. "Any chance I could get more of that very fine pain medicine?"

Pursing her lips like a prissy schoolteacher, she nodded. "I suppose that could be managed, but I'll be sure to ration it this time."

Theatrically, he bowed his head and crossed his hands

over his heart. "Cruelty, thy name is woman."

"Hmph. It's better than you deserve, Pinkerton."

"Oh, so now that it's certain I'll live, you're back to calling me Pinkerton."

"*Sí*," she said with no hint of expression.

Her nonchalance didn't fool him. "And is *that* what you called me when I was delirious?" he said, challenging her to remember her softer side.

"You don't remember?" She straightened his covers. "That's unfortunate." She turned to leave, then glanced over her shoulder and favored him with an arched smile. "Maybe it'll come to you."

"Ugh!" He grabbed the smaller icepack from the floor and tossed it at her shapely ass.

"You missed," she said with a laugh, scurrying down the hallway.

Damn. As seductive as she was aggravating. Too bad he was already in love with her. A woman who had every reason to hate him. And one who had no intention of ever allowing another man into her life. Frowning, he rubbed his itching chin between his thumb and forefinger. If he didn't shave soon, he'd have a full beard.

Marooned. Injured. Living the life of a virtual vagabond, he just never counted on falling in love with anyone—much less the subject of his investigation. That pretty much settled it. His life was fast on the road to hell in a hand-basket.

Natalia stopped in the hallway to catch her breath, leaning against the cool adobe wall. *Dios.* Jared's little-boy appeal hadn't gone away when he awakened. She could still see the glint of childlike mischief in his steel-gray gaze, as well as the deep hurt he hid so well behind his ruggedly handsome *macho* exterior. Relieved that his fever had broken but bone-tired, she wanted nothing more than to crawl into bed and sleep for at least a week.

But such blissful rest wasn't what the new day held. Her stomach growled, reminding her of the animals in the stable. They hadn't eaten either. And there was the cow to be milked.

Dress. Brave the icy wind and snow. Feed the animals. Muck the stable. Bring in more wood. Back to the ranch house. Fix breakfast. See to Jared's injured leg.

Dios, the cold and the never-ending work was wearing her down. Her feet felt rooted to the floor. Slowly, she slid down the wall until...

She shook herself awake and stiffened her legs and back. *No, keep moving. Don't give in.* Trudging into the kitchen, she grabbed a slice of bread from the keeper. She buttered it, even opened her mouth to bite into the yeasty goodness—

No. She shook her head and carried the bread to Jared, who looked up from fumbling with the cold pack on his leg. "This should hold you until I get back from the stable; then I'll—"

"Forget about me. Talia, you're pale. Dammit, you're on the verge of collapse." He swung his good leg off the chaise and set it on the floor. "Where's the cane? I've lain around here long enough." He threw the melted pack on the floor and, using both hands, gingerly lifted his injured leg off the chaise. "The cane?"

"No!" Did he think she couldn't cope with a little extra work? "You need another day with that leg elevated. I'll take care of the animals, fix breakfast, and then I'll lie down for a while."

He shook his head. "No. I can hobble around with the cane." He looked from side to side, his gaze darting around the room. "Where'd you hide the damned thing?"

Natalia rolled her eyes. Honestly, men... "Under the chaise, next to your left foot. If it were a rattler, you'd be a dead man."

A little sheepishly, he grinned up at her. "So I see." He bent over, snatched the ebony cane and gave it a twirl. "Very distinguished," he said, then stroked his mustache with a dramatic flourish.

Stubborn oaf, yet charming. She couldn't help but smile at his antics. "All right. If you insist on getting up, maybe you could manage breakfast while I'm outside?"

He raised his chin and glanced down his nose in a haughty manner. "I'll have you know that on my travels, I've cooked over an open fire many a time."

She set her hands on her hips. "Well, I hope you're not planning on starting an open fire in my home, Pinkerton."

"Gah! There you go, *Pinkerton* again."

"It's what you are." Best not forget it, either—no matter how boyish and charming he was.

"It's true. I came here under false pretenses. But I don't believe for a minute you had your husband murdered." His gaze held hers. For once, his expression was unclouded by any attempt to dissemble. "For the life of me, can't think why you didn't. Men have been murdered for less."

His words touched and chilled her at the same time.

"Purely and simply, I'm not a murderer. If I were, I would've already gotten rid of you."

"May not be so easy to get rid of, Talia." He burst out laughing; then his features contorted.

"You're still in pain, aren't you?"

"Not like I was yesterday. A shot of whiskey wouldn't go amiss though."

Grinning, Natalia shoved the bread in his face. "Eat this first. I'd hate to have a drunk set my kitchen on fire."

"Yes, ma'am." He took the bread from her and took the first bite. With his mouth still full, he mumbled, "This is the best bread I've ever eaten."

She laughed. "You're just hungry." Heading toward the door, she stopped sharply and turned. In as innocent a tone as she could muster, she asked, "Do you need my assistance in the water closet?"

An expression of horror crossed his handsome face. "No!"

She chuckled, having just made the suggestion in the hopes of being rewarded with such a reaction. "All right, then. I'll leave you to your morning ablutions with your modesty intact." Served him right for being such a prude about his bodily needs when he was anything but a prude in bed.

Back to the kitchen, where she sliced another piece of bread and buttered it. She groaned with pleasure when she took a bite. Quickly, she finished breaking her fast. It would have to do for now.

Unable to avoid going outside any longer, she pulled the heavy overcoat from the hook by the door and shoved a Stetson on her head. On opening the door, she found a very different landscape. Snow had stopped falling, and the sun shone with a blinding brilliance across the fields. Melting ice steadily dripped from the edges of the tile roof. Wind blew from the south. Just maybe the snow would melt before winter set in for good.

But then Jared would leave.

As much as he'd angered her with his deception, she would miss his company. Miss arguing with him. Miss joking with him. And especially having him in her bed. What a revelation it was to have a lover who knew how to pleasure a woman when she'd had so little in her marriage. Hah! She'd experienced none there at all.

While she had trusted him with her body, trusting him with her heart was another matter. Did she dare take his words about working the ranch alongside her seriously? Could she trust him to keep his word and not abandon her if he grew tired of ranch life?

Crossing the courtyard, she easily made her way through the trench to the stable. Outside the stable door, she could hear the fretful lowing of the milk cow and impatient neighing of the two horses. Poor creatures needed exercise. But that would have to wait.

Chapter Fourteen

Before tackling breakfast on the cookstove, Jared washed his face and cast a long glance at Montrose's straight razor, then finger-combed his hair and headed to the kitchen.

Leaning on the serpent-headed cane in front of the cookstove, he shook his head and frowned. "Dang." Building a fire was simple enough, but regulating it so that it would cook the food and not burn it was another issue. An open campfire was much less complicated.

He opened the iron door. "No time like the present." He pulled wood from the basket by the cookstove and thrust it inside. Using a safety match, he lit a twisted piece of newspaper and set the wood alight. He waited until the fire was established, then shut and secured the door.

By poking around the icebox and the pantry, he located eggs, bacon and a heavy iron skillet. He placed bacon in the skillet and set it on the stove plate. While he waited for the bacon to fry, he found a bowl and broke five eggs into it with only a minimum of shell. He yanked open several drawers before he found a fork to whip the eggs.

Yeah, he could do a fine breakfast. Biscuits surely would

be nice, but he didn't have a clue how to bake anything like that. There was still half a loaf of bread in the keeper. That would have to do.

Trying to ignore the pain in his leg, he hummed while he whipped the eggs and listened to the sizzling and popping of the bacon while it cooked. He nosed over the skillet. Time to flip. Now where— Hell, he'd just use the fork.

Bacon was about to burn. Stove was too hot. He reached for the skillet to pull it off the stove. "Damn!" Should've wrapped the handle with a towel. Close call. He almost dropped their breakfast. Now his hand was burnt. Great. Fucking great.

Carefully, he grabbed a towel and folded it, then set the skillet to the side and turned the strips over. Grease popped on the back of his hand, and he almost dropped half their breakfast again. "Crap!" He sucked the burned spot. Ought to put some butter on it, but he was pulled in too many directions. Time to take up the bacon. By now it was—um, crisp.

Still edible. He'd eaten worse.

He found a clean dishtowel and set the bacon on it to drain. When Talia returned from the stable, he'd cook the eggs. No point in serving his hostess burnt bacon *and* rubbery eggs. She made cooking breakfast look simple as could be. Well, it wasn't—not by a long shot—not on an unfamiliar cooking implement and with a bum leg to boot.

He limped over to a chair and sat, then pulled another chair around to face him, using it to prop his bad leg. "Whew." He could take it easy until Talia returned. Now where was—

In his poking around, he hadn't discovered Montrose's liquor stash, and he could really use a pick-me-up. Then he spied the coffeepot on the back of the stove. Coffee. Yeah, coffee would do. Talia would appreciate a hot cup when she returned from the stable where she was doing the chores he ought to be doing.

He moved his bad leg from the chair and hobbled over to the stove. The heat from the stove lent the kitchen a homey atmosphere. Spending the rest of his life here with Talia didn't seem like such a bad idea. Using water from the snow Talia had melted, he dipped the coffee pot into the large copper kettle.

Now where was the coffee? Damn. Why couldn't anything be easy? He limped into the pantry and inspected several containers. Finally he found the coffee. Now at least he could brew her a cup of coffee and earn his keep while she was outside doing a man's work. No matter what she said about her strength and ability to stand alongside any man, he'd clearly seen how exhausted she was from watching over him all night.

Not since his mother had anyone shown him as much care as Talia had. Talia, the wild, temperamental and passionate woman he'd always dreamed of but never thought existed.

After setting the coffeepot onto the stove, he shuffled back to his chair, leaned back and waited for the coffee to percolate.

His eyelids grew heavy. About to nod off, he shook himself awake in time to see Talia dragging a load of firewood across the courtyard. He got to his feet to open the door and motioned with a come-here gesture. "Let me.

Nothing wrong with my arms."

She shot him a grateful smile but shook her head. "Wait until I get to the door; otherwise you might slip."

He nodded but chafed at watching her small frame tugging the heavy load of firewood. "It's stopped snowing," he said, amazed he hadn't noticed earlier.

"*Sí.* The wind has died down, and the sun is out, and it's melting ice and snow off the roof."

Was it possible the weather would improve enough for him to get back to town? Damn. He didn't want to leave her, and just how much he didn't want that shook him. "But there's still no way to travel safely. I don't know the area well enough to risk endangering my horse."

"No." Talia gave a quick shake of her head. "It wouldn't be safe. Not yet. Not at all."

Jared shouldered the firewood and deposited several logs into the basket beside the stove. He carried the rest to the bedroom, then limped back to the kitchen to finish preparing their breakfast. Surely he couldn't muck up a simple meal.

Natalia headed for the water closet. Freshening her appearance and getting rid of the stable smell would do a lot to improve her mood. After removing her odorous outer garments, she splashed cold water on her face. From Reginald's chifforobe she pulled out a clean flannel shirt and a pair of denim trousers. They would do until the weather moderated. Then back to her bedroom, where she ran a brush through her hair, twisting it into a low knot on her neck and securing it with hairpins.

Heading back to the kitchen, she inhaled the aromas of coffee and burnt bacon. Even so, her stomach growled and her mouth watered. No matter how bad Jared's cooking, she was starved and wouldn't say a word about his skills.

"Now you sit," she ordered. "I'll pour the coffee and put the food on the table. It smells wonderful."

Jared snorted. "You must be starving. I have to warn you the bacon's on the crisp side, but I managed to keep it from scorching completely by picking up the skillet and burning my hand instead."

"Oh no. Let me see."

He held out his hand, palm up. A blister had already formed. "It's not so bad," he said, wincing.

"Ice." Natalia turned, intending to scoop up some ice or snow from the courtyard.

He snatched her wrist, stopping her forward movement. "Is your intention to pack my entire body in ice?"

"Don't be absurd." She gave him a teasing smile. "Just the injured parts."

"All right. More ice. But how I'm going to get around with a burnt hand and a broken leg..." He shrugged, holding up his hands in a gesture of surrender.

"Never fear, Pinkerton." She stroked his cheek. "I'll see to your needs."

His dark brows rose. "To which needs might you be referring?"

"Why, your health needs, of course. Speaking of which, it's time for another dose of willow-bark tea."

He frowned, reminding her again of the little boy she'd watched over last night. "Nasty stuff. Won't it ruin my appetite?"

Laughing, she turned to go to the pantry. "Nothing's going to ruin your appetite." Not if she could help it. She located the second dose of the medicinal tea on the table where she'd left it to steep. Might as well prepare the next dose now.

She returned. "Dose number two. Drink it all. And don't complain."

He frowned, but took the cup, swallowed the contents, then grimaced. "Gah! Awful."

She set a cup of fresh coffee before him. "Wash it down with this." Then she placed a plateful of scrambled eggs and bacon on the table. "Let's eat. I'm starving."

After sitting, she bit into a piece of burnt bacon and chewed the crunchy meat. Putting on her best smile, she said, "This is really good."

"Cut the crap, Talia. I know it's bad. But I've eaten worse. At least the eggs turned out all right."

She nodded and quietly removed a piece of eggshell to the side of her place. "*Sí*, light and fluffy." Truthfully the eggs were wonderful—bits of shell and all. But even a raw prairie dog would taste like heaven right now.

"I admit it. I'm not much of a cook." Jared waved a piece of bacon under her nose. "Tonight I'll see to the animals, and you'll cook."

Natalia straightened her back and gave him her most regal stare. "Really? Are you ordering me around in my own kitchen?"

"Don't think of it as my ordering you around. I know you hate that."

He thought he knew her so well after such a short acquaintance. Involuntarily, her chin jutted. "And just *how* should I think of it?"

He calmly buttered a piece of bread, then said, "Think of it as the common-sense solution to our problems."

"Because I don't want to see you injured further, I'm not using common sense? I think you have it backward." She took in a deep breath, then let it out with a huff. "Am I merely being nonsensical, or is it that I'm just an emotional woman while you're the logical male?"

He stopped eating long enough to say, "You have me all wrong, Talia. My eyes tell me you're about to drop in your tracks. I said it before and I'll say it again. *You* need rest."

His beautiful eyes saw too much. Truthfully he was right about her needing rest. "I'll rest today," she said with a sigh, "but let us discuss it again this evening. A day's rest will put me right. And another day with your leg elevated wouldn't hurt you either."

His gray gaze from beneath thick, dark lashes was as warm as a summer's afternoon. He gave her a wide, knowing grin. "Perhaps we could rest together?" Never breaking eye contact, he picked up his coffee cup and took a sip.

Rest together indeed. She touched her lips with her napkin, hiding her smile. "I'm not sure we would find much rest in such a situation."

Letting out a hearty laugh, he set his coffee cup on the table. "Dear Talia, you overestimate my powers of recovery."

"I have seen evidence of your recuperative powers..." She paused for effect then continued, "On more than one occasion."

"Indeed. And I would hate to disappoint the *señora* with

a less than satisfactory performance." With that devilish little-boy grin, he crunched down on the last strip of bacon, cleaning his plate. "*Gracias*, Talia, for the food and the pleasure of your company. You're a most gracious hostess."

Reaching across the table, he covered her hand with his large, calloused one. Her arm jerked, responding to the rush of heat from his simple gesture. His touch made her want to melt into his arms again. To feel the exhilaration of heightened senses while they rode to the brink and exploded into ecstasy. His skin against hers, each caress sending a curl of pleasure to her core. His hard cock driving into the recesses of her body.

Her breathing grew ragged as the images flew through her mind.

"Talia?"

Jared's concerned tone drew her back from her brief reverie. Biting her bottom lip, she regained her composure.

"You were remembering our being together, weren't you?" His tone, no longer concerned but instead soft and seductive, brought a smile to her mouth.

"*Sí*," she said with some hesitation. "You're a wonderful lover." Never would she have ever referred to sexual matters to Reginald. Such things "*weren't fit for breakfast conversation*" was what he told her the one time she tried to speak of it. "Your touch brought it all back."

Still somewhat shy of talking about lovemaking, she rose from the table. "I'll bring in more snow to heat. It won't be enough for a true bath, but you can freshen up using Reginald's shaving things."

Grinning, Jared rubbed his chin. "Yeah. Could use a shave. Wouldn't want to rub a certain someone's delicate parts the wrong way."

Heat suffused her neck and cheeks. She turned away to keep him from seeing her sudden embarrassment. No matter how natural their lovemaking was, talking about it so openly and away from the bedroom was too new an experience. Yet she found the prospect pleasurable.

"No, we wouldn't want that," she finally managed to say. At the same time, she removed the lid from the large copper kettle. Rushing out into the courtyard with the kettle, she relished the cold. While the sun was beaming down and had already melted the ice and snow from the roof, it was still cold with the accumulation of waist-high drifts. A brisk wind from the south had picked up. *Bueno.* Maybe it would bring a brief spell of warmer weather before the long dark days of winter set in for good.

Calm down, she told herself, as she knelt and rubbed a handful of snow on her face to cool her burning cheeks. She quickly filled the kettle with snow, piling it high, then rose. Sadly, if the weather improved enough, Jared would have no reason to stay. As startling as her feelings for Jared were, she'd grown accustomed to having him at her side.

When she turned and saw Jared standing in the doorway with a wide grin across his handsome face, she tucked her head and brushed past him.

"What's your hurry?" he drawled lazily.

"Hurry? No hurry." She shook her head. "Just wanted to get inside out of the cold."

"The kettle's too heavy for you. Let me do it," he said. Taking the kettle from her trembling hands, he then hobbled over to the cookstove and set it on a burner plate.

Grateful, she nodded. Back inside the kitchen, it was

warm compared to the courtyard. Or maybe the warmth resulted from Jared's nearness and the heated desire roiling through her entire body. Desire so strong her very insides quivered.

With a small sigh, she started to clear the breakfast dishes from the table, but Jared stopped her with a look. "No. Off to bed with you. I'll clean up this mess, shave, and then I'll join you."

Jared's hand at the small of her back gently nudged her toward the bedroom. Truth be told, she was exhausted beyond anything she'd ever known. Too tired to resist, she craved the warmth of his touch. "*Sí.*"

On their reaching her bedchamber, she shivered, then rubbed her arms. "It's cooler in here."

He nodded. "Fire's died down. I'll stir it up after I get you into bed."

Permitting herself a small smile, she met his gaze. "I believe you have a habit of stirring things up. Isn't that what happened the last time you put me to bed?"

"Ma'am, who am I to disagree with such a purty lady," he said, affecting a cowhand's drawl. A seductive smile played about his lips. "If you say I stirred things up, then I surely accomplished what I set out to do."

She tucked her head, hiding a smile. After sitting on the bed, she tugged her boots off and yawned. She stretched and watched while Jared limped over to the fireplace, picked up the poker and stirred the fire into a blaze that took the chill from the room. Then he added more wood, ensuring her comfort while she rested.

"Lie down. I'll cover you up." His tone was deep and thick with emotion or pain. His Adam's apple bobbed as he swallowed.

She lay down and snuggled into the warm coverlet he spread over her. His tenderness was so unexpected her throat ached. "You're hurting, aren't you? Have more of the whiskey. There's another bottle of his best in Reginald's bedchamber...the bottom drawer of his wardrobe. He never knew I was aware of his secret cache."

"I'll find it." He straightened and rubbed his chin. "But first, shut your eyes and forget about me. I'm a grown man. I can manage on my own long enough for you to get some sleep."

"You're sure?" She pushed up on her elbow. "Don't forget the next dose of willow-bark tea." She shook her head. "No, never mind. I won't sleep that long. I just need a quick nap." Yawning, she rested her head on the pillow, closed her eyes and slid into sleep.

***

Jared leaned over her body and smiled as he watched exhaustion claim her quicker than he'd thought possible. She'd had a grueling twenty-four hours, watching over him during his bout of fever. Between the chills and the night sweats, he'd sensed her comforting presence but lacked the energy to reassure her he was all right.

A shrill whistle snapped him back to the present. The smaller kettle was boiling. Now he could shave and clean up a bit. He leaned on the cane and hobbled back to the kitchen. The remains of their breakfast had congealed on their plates. Oh well. He shrugged. Cleaning up the kitchen could wait.

The sooner he shaved, the sooner he could snuggle beside Talia.

Chapter Fifteen

"Mm," Talia moaned, spooning deeper in the warm embrace of two strong arms. A hard cock poked her backside, and a warm hand insinuated itself between her legs. "I thought you were going to let me sleep awhile." She let out a sigh of pure contentment.

A deep chuckle emanated from her bed partner. "I did. You slept all day, like the dead. I didn't have the heart to awaken you, so I shaved, had a wash, and then, when I couldn't put it off any longer, I cleaned up the kitchen. A first for me, I assure you."

She sighed. "I'm sure it was. And now with nothing else to do, you decided to waken me and have your reward for good behavior."

"Ah, but the reward is all yours." His fingers slipped in and out of her cleft.

Her thighs tight against his hand, she squirmed, enjoying the intimacy of his every touch. "Very sure of your charms, aren't you, sir?"

"Did your little nap"—he rapidly flicked her clit and eased his cock between her legs—"erase your memory of our time together?"

"Not at all." She reached between her legs and grasped the large head of his cock, rubbing it in her juices and centering it as he thrust inside her. "While I slept, I even dreamt about our lovemaking." Her inner walls stretched, then contracted as she met him stroke for stroke.

Her heart swelled with emotion as he made love to her lying on their sides.

He grasped her breasts, cupping them, then tweaking the nipples into tight pearls of sensation while he assaulted her neck with kisses. Her body burned, seemed to glow and arch toward the sky. Her voice raspy, she cried out his name while an explosion of the purest pleasure she'd ever known rocked through her body.

He filled her core to the depths, his breath harsh and hot in her ear. His groan of release was low, long and hoarse. "Talia. Talia." He moaned her name over and over.

If only she could lie like this forever. If he would never leave her. What would life be like if she always had his arms around her, protecting her from the outside world? Unable to restrain it, she let a sigh of regret escape.

Jared tenderly brushed the hair from her forehead. "What's wrong?" He levered up onto one elbow.

"Nothing." Reluctant to move and sever the bond that made them one, she shook her head. "I'm so content. If we only—" She broke off, not wanting to make impossible demands and ruin the sensual spell of their lovemaking.

"If we only what?"

Yawning, she propped on one elbow and shook her hair loose. "Never mind. It was nothing."

"Tell me." He wove his fingers through her hair, straightening the tangles. "You know your hair's like silk," he murmured.

"How's your leg?" she asked in an attempt to divert his attention. What would be the point of making her pathetic vulnerability so obvious? He would move on when the weather improved. And she might as well just get used to the idea.

"Aches some." His gaze locked with hers. "Don't change the subject. What was the big sigh about?"

"It wasn't a big sigh." Tossing her hair, she gave a furious huff. "Anyway, you're making a mountain out of a— whatever!" She scooted away from him and felt the loss of their connection. It wasn't a mere physical connection of the flesh but one of the spirit. At least that was how it seemed to her. For men, sexual congress was all about the physical. She'd learned that much from her not-so-dearly-departed spouse.

Shivering, she swung her feet to the floor, then wrapped the coverlet around her body and rushed over to sit on the settee, closer to the fire.

"No fair," Jared said. "You took all the warmth with you."

Without turning, she heard the bed creak, and a second later felt the heat of his body behind her.

"Come back to bed. Your feet will freeze on the cold tiles."

"I'm all right," she said, trying to ignore the pounding of her heart and the heat. The heat that burned inside her, hotter than the fire blazing in the hearth. The need to lose herself in his embrace.

"Then why are you sitting in front of the fire shivering?" He placed his hands on her shoulders, then gathered her so close to his chest she could feel his heart hammering in time with hers.

"What's wrong?" he asked. "What have I done?"

His tenderness was too much to bear. Tears stung her eyes, threatening to spill down her cheeks. Hurriedly, she blinked them away. *Take control.* "Nothing." She inhaled and pasted on a satisfied smile, then turned to face him. "You've attended to my needs quite well. No woman could ask for a better lover."

At Talia's words, Jared straightened. Stung—hell no— more than stung, he was damned insulted by her lack of sentiment. As if he were nothing more than a hired gigolo. After the way she'd cared for him, and he her, he expected more—a hell of a lot more. "Happy to be of service, *Señora* Montrose."

If he could've gotten on his horse and ridden out, this would be that moment. Anger roiled through him like heat off desert sand. He clenched his fists at his side. His chest rose and fell as he sucked in the cold air, fueling his rage.

Her eyes widened in fear, and her hands came up, guarding her face as her body shrank from contact. A wave of shame swept through him. Never had he struck a woman in anger. And he wasn't about to make the cowering woman in front of him the first. She'd been hit before—no doubt about it. The signs were all there. Here he was with fisted hands, as if he were an uncivilized brute, ready to strike a woman who'd only hurt him with words, never in deed.

Shaking his head, he willed his fists to relax, turned, grabbed his cane and limped from the room. Before he closed the door behind him, he heard her let out a sigh. His throat clenched. That he scared her hurt. Hurt him.

Leaning against the cool adobe wall outside her bedchamber, he heard her crying—no, sobbing. Why? He hadn't touched her. Nor had he given more than a bitter response, the result of the pain her words caused. He hadn't attacked her at all.

Talia wasn't some fragile debutante who'd swoon at the faintest of insults. No, for his however brief show of anger to upset her so... He'd scared her, pure and simple. The disparity of their strength alone was enough to frighten any woman. Had he lost control, he could've crushed her fragile frame. No matter how strong a woman she was, she was still vulnerable to the greater strength of a man.

He swallowed the bitter taste shame left in his mouth. If he didn't get outside soon... If the snow didn't melt soon... What if they were trapped all winter? The house was already closing in on him, smothering him.

He hobbled into the kitchen, grabbed the coat off the hook and slid his arms inside. Without buttoning it, he struggled outside into the walled garden. Not that there was anything to see of the garden. Shading his eyes from the bright snow, he turned and glanced upward at the tiled roof. The day's sun had melted most of the ice and snow. The sides of the trench to the stable were no longer waist-high. In the far distance, he easily made out the two flat-topped mountains.

Sucking in a lungful of crisp, cold air, he instantly regretted it when the burn hit. But dammit, he needed the fresh air to clear his head. Might as well see to the horses. If the sun would come out tomorrow like it had today, he might be able to find the route back to town.

But that would mean leaving Talia alone. And after he left, what if the weather worsened again? How would she manage without his help?

He didn't want to think about all that could go wrong with a woman alone. What if she were injured? No one might find her for days. How long would it take her ranch hands to return to the hacienda if the snow was as bad in town as it was here?

No, he wouldn't leave her. He couldn't. To tell the truth, and in spite of all the reasons to the contrary, he didn't want to.

Chapter Sixteen

As soon as Jared shut the door, Natalia broke down and sobbed. Seeing the rage written over his features as well as the tension in his body brought back the two times, early in her marriage, when Reginald had beaten her into submission. The first time when she'd refused to let him take her from behind like an animal in the field. He'd won that round. A second time, one of his friends from back East had shown her too much attention over dinner. Later that night in her bedchamber, he'd beaten her just to show she belonged to him and he could do as he damned well pleased with her.

After that, she took to carrying a knife and practiced throwing it until her aim was deadly accurate. She allowed him to see her new skill. He paled and swallowed as if her knife were already in his throat. But he never beat her again.

However, humiliation came in many forms, and Reginald was expert in delivering all of them. But she was tough. Humiliation she could handle.

And now she harbored in her heart love for the man who could conceivably think her capable of killing her late husband. And truth be told, she was.

Bastardo. Her only regret was that someone else had killed him first.

The rise of anger stopped her tears. She calmly rose from the chaise, quickly dressed and then splashed the icy-cold water from the basin onto her face. Maybe the cold would banish the signs of her crying bout.

She paused at the door, then opened it, expecting to find Jared lurking about. He was neither in the drawing room nor the kitchen. The heavy coat he'd worn was missing from the hook. It was too early to see after the horses. Where could he have gone?

She peered out the window. The snow drifts weren't nearly as high as they had been. The realization that her hurtful words had driven him away gave her a sinking feeling in the pit of her belly. Maybe he decided she was such a *bruja* he might as well take his chances on finding his way back to town. He'd left her to her own devices. Just as she deserved. Her mouth dried as the reality of being all alone hit her.

Why had she been so cruel? She'd said such uncaring things. True, she'd thought to ease the pain of their eventual parting, but instead she'd made it worse.

Outside, the bright sunshine underscored the frigid cold inside the house. Unable to stop shivering, she hugged herself. Tears stung her eyes, but she blinked them back. The least he could've done before he left was bring in more firewood.

Stop it. She wasn't some delicate ninny from New York City. No, she was a strong and resourceful woman of the West. Born and bred to this hard life, she'd be fine. She would!

First, she'd bring in more firewood. She yanked her coat from the hook and had started to put it on when a face appeared in the window. She gasped. Her hand went to her throat.

Jared...loaded down with firewood.

Relief rushed through her, weakening her knees. Hah! Strong and resourceful—right. And ready to pass out with gratitude because he hadn't deserted her after all.

She opened the door and was met by a blast of cold air. "I feared you'd gone." No. She'd blurted out the words, words that revealed her vulnerability.

"I considered it," he said with little expression. He stumbled over the doorsill, almost dropping the wood.

Without hesitating, she reached to steady him. Not that he really needed it. "Careful." She stepped back to let him limp by her. "I'm glad you didn't leave," she admitted.

"Really?" Still with no observable sign of his feelings, he bent over and set the wood into the basket by the cookstove. He straightened up, then faced her, his mouth set in a stern line. "What's the matter? Dawn on you what could go wrong if I weren't here?"

Arrogant man. "Maybe..." She raised her chin a notch. "But I'm not the one limping."

"You could've been," he said, his tone as dry as the summer desert. He removed his gloves and stuffed them in his pockets.

She clasped her hands in front of her, mainly to keep them from trembling. "I didn't mean it."

"Oh, so I'm not an attentive lover after all?" His steel-gray gaze locked with hers. "You're saying I didn't meet your needs?"

Natalia stamped her foot. "*Dios*! That's not what I meant."

"Then spell it out, *señora*." Hands on his hips, he stared, still not giving away what was on his mind.

"You've become more than someone who meets my needs," she began. Could the man be any more infuriating? He wasn't giving an inch. Letting him know how she truly felt gave him too much power. Finally, she managed to say, "*Sí*, you mean more to me than that. I certainly didn't mean to offend you."

"That's exactly what you meant to do. And it worked. Why try to drive me away? Am I that...?"

She shushed him, placing her finger to his lips. "Because you'll be leaving anyway, as soon as the weather improves. Will you not?"

His expression softened. He took her fingers, kissed them. "I'm sorry I scared you. I've never hit a woman. I don't intend to start now." He pulled her close to his chest. "As for leaving, don't know how I could. You might be with child."

Natalia's heart lightened at the thought of having his baby, a son who would grow strong and tall like his father. "That's not enough. I wouldn't use a child to bind you to me." She nestled into his strong shoulder.

He kissed the top of her head, then smiled. "You wouldn't have to. I'd never desert you or my child."

"But your employer, Pinkerton, what would happen?"

"Nothing. I'd just wire them that I quit. I could stay here with you. There's no one back East who gives a tinker's damn what I do. My father gave up on me years ago. My mother's gone. My only sibling—well, let's just say he was likely happy to see the last of me."

Dios. He was as alone in the world as she. The thought saddened her, but it was a bond they shared whether or not there was a child from their union. "But won't they just send someone else? Reginald's father won't give up that easily."

"Then I'll have to clear your good name and to hell with Montrose." He held her as if he would never let her go and pressed a light kiss on top of her head. Then he pushed her away to arm's length, his gaze locked with hers. "Damn, but you're the most beautiful woman I've ever known. I won't ever leave you."

Instinctively, her hands went to her belly. "Other than the first time, Reginald never took me the *normal* way. He didn't want to risk having a half-Mexican brat. What if there is no child? What if I'm barren?"

He smiled. Emotions glimmered in his gaze as he watched her lovingly. And even though he'd told her he loved her before, it'd been in the throes of passion or while he was inebriated. Could she trust him now?

"Not even then." He brushed a strand of hair behind her ear and lowered his lips to hers. His kiss was tender, then demanding as she opened to him. Her tongue swept his, challenging him. Her arms went around his neck. He picked her up and set her on the pine table.

Sí, she would give him her love, her heart, her body and soul.

He unbuttoned her shirt, then undid her trousers, pulling them off her legs. She kicked them the rest of the way off and reached for the front of his denims. Together they struggled with his buttons until she found his jutting hard cock. When his warm flesh pressed to her already moist cleft, she thought this was surely heaven.

He pulled her hips to the edge of the table, and her legs encircled his waist. He thrust home, hard and swift. She gasped for air while her body adjusted to his breadth and length. Clasping the end of the table for leverage, she arched her hips and met him stroke for stroke. Sweet strokes. Pounding strokes. Punishing strokes.

Jared braced his hands on either side of Talia as she locked her ankles around his waist. Unable to believe the hot sweetness of their loving, he kissed her neck and nibbled his way down to her lush breasts. He snaked his hands beneath her woolen underwear and raked the garment up to reveal her chocolate-brown nipples already beaded into tight nubs.

He sucked one, then gasped when an arrow of need shot straight to his groin, making him feel like he would burst any second. Too late to slow down now. No way to make it last.

No need. Talia was already trembling in his arms. Her breathing was ragged in his ear as she cried his name. He gave one final thrust and shot over the precipice with her. He gently cradled her head in his hands and kissed her sweet mouth. As if he could've ever left her and given up the sweet loving he'd found in her arms. Never.

Her hands played under his shirt along the muscles of his back. "You're burning up."

He nodded. "You're telling me."

"No. I mean your fever's back." She pushed up on her

elbows and stared at him, her brows pulled together in a frown. "When was the last time you drank the willow-bark tea?"

Jared thought for a second, then shrugged. "I don't know. This morning?"

She squirmed, trying to get off the table. "You must have another dose now."

"Now?" He smiled down at her. "I was kind of enjoying this. Weren't you?"

She rolled her eyes. "Of course I was, but—"

He cut off her protest with another kiss, then relented as she shook her head. "All right. All right. I'll drink more of that nasty concoction of yours. But then—"

"No but-then anything. You're going back to bed—"

"Okay by me. That's what was on my mind anyway."

"None of that until your fever goes down," she said as sternly as any schoolmarm. "Go! Go on." She waved him away.

He gave a frustrated huff, then pulled back, reluctantly breaking the physical bond between them.

Still frowning, Talia slipped off the table, grabbed up her trousers and redressed while he buttoned his pants and shirt. "I'll get the tea," she said and headed to the pantry.

Come to think of it, his leg was throbbing more than it had been. Guess making love with a bum leg while standing at the kitchen table wasn't the greatest idea he'd ever had. Just seemed like it at the time. He smiled, the intensity of their encounter still fresh in his mind's eye.

He could never get enough of Talia if he lived to be a hundred. Ah, to have her in his bed night after night and wake up to her sweet loving morning after morning. Life couldn't be any better. Certainly better than the life of a Pinkerton agent. Alone, always on the move. No home. No roots. Once, those were the very assets he treasured about the job. Until now.

Talia's rushing in from the pantry broke his reverie. "Here." She held out the cup of the noxious brew. "Drink it now."

Grudgingly, he took the cup, but he couldn't keep from smiling. "You're a bossy female if ever there was one."

"You have no idea." Hands on her hips, she stood staring at him with a stern expression. "Now drink it down."

"Couldn't you add some honey? Y'know, sweeten it a bit."

"I'll show you sweet if you don't swallow it right now."

"All right. You win." He downed the bitter tea in one go but gasped from the taste. "Makes me want to wash my mouth out with soap. That's how bad the stuff is."

He watched her struggle not to laugh. She held her sides, and her mouth contorted, but she finally broke down and laughed.

As soon as his woman—yes, he thought of her that way—could compose herself, she said, pointing theatrically, "Sorry, but you're not out of the woods yet. Now get your very fine body to bed."

Relentless—yes, she was. And she was his. He meant to keep her that way forever.

Chapter Seventeen

Finally, Natalia had Jared settled in her bed with his injured leg propped on two pillows. The aggravating man insisted on tending to the fires in the cookstove and her bedchamber before he would agree to go to bed. Once there, he consented to her rewrapping his leg and covering it with another snowpack.

Gazing up at her, he folded his arms across his chest. "You know, this wasn't quite what I had in mind."

"I know exactly what you had in mind, but this is what *I* had in mind." She bent over and straightened the coverlet. "You still have a lot of swelling, but it's not as bad as it was."

"Goes to show you make an excellent nursemaid," he told her with a cheeky wiggle of his dark brows.

She set her hands on her hips and told him firmly, "I'll have you know, women out here are strong and can do just about anything, including our men's jobs."

He nodded slowly and solemnly. "You'll get no argument from me, Talia. I'm a believer."

She shook her finger in his face but had trouble hiding her grin. "If you weren't so poorly, I'd smack your cheeks."

"Poorly? I'll have *you* know I did a damned good job...for an injured man."

"Indeed you did at that." Her mouth tugged into a smile she could no longer hide. "A very damned good job."

A sound she'd gradually become aware of while getting Jared situated now increased in volume. "The wind," she said, "do you hear it?"

Frowning, he came up on one elbow. "Hope we're not in for more snow."

She rushed to the window and parted the heavy draperies. She used her hand to wipe off a rime of frost. "The sun is still shining. No snow, but the wind's blowing from the southwest, and it's clearing some of the drifts. I can almost make out where the road is."

Jared rubbed his chin. "That settles it. I'm going to try to get into town tomorrow."

"No." Natalia shook her head. "Why would you risk it? Something could easily happen. Your leg—it's not up to riding...surely?"

"I need to telegraph my employers to let them know what I've been up to. And I need to see the sheriff, again. I checked in with him before coming out here."

News to her. "Really? Just in case I murdered you and did away with your body?"

"Didn't know what I was riding into," he admitted somewhat shyly. "Never hurts to have someone at your back."

She sat at the foot of the bed. "Don't you think the sheriff will be too busy with the blizzard to notice you're not around?"

"Got to admit he wasn't too pleased about my being in

town. Local lawmen tend to get a little testy when the Pinkertons get involved." He stared out the window, his movements restless as if he was anxious to leave. "If it was up to the sheriff, he'd just as soon I hightailed it out of town and the sooner, the better. Said I was wasting my time."

"I am very glad he did not insist you leave."

"Wouldn't have done him any good. I mean to finish my assignment."

His bald statement pierced her heart. She rose, ready to defend herself. "You still think I had my husband killed?" How could he? After all they'd been through, how was it possible he continued to think of her as a mere assignment?

"No, but there are a few questions I need answered about this Juan Ojeda, the fellow who did kill him."

"Like what?" All right, she needed to give him a chance to explain. He was being thorough. That was all it was. Surely.

"Like was he a stranger in town? If he wasn't, who did he work for? How did he get away without being caught? Little things I need to know to clear you."

Perhaps his declarations of love were really true. Otherwise, he wouldn't care whether she was cleared or not. She reached forward and caressed his cheek. "That's very sweet. But when the sheriff was here, he didn't seem like he thought I had anything to do with Reginald's death. It was just a barroom brawl that ended in murder."

"Granted it seems pretty straightforward. But you had plenty of reason to hate your husband, and no doubt you could find the money, since you did your husband's books.

And you could've hired Ojeda to make it look like something other than premeditated murder."

Her chin dropped, and she put her trembling hand to her mouth. "But I thought you—"

"Hold on. I don't think you had anything to do with it. But I have to look at the situation like a lawman would. Figure out what the local sheriff or a marshal would need to know in order to find the truth."

Getting weak in the knees, she sat on the bed. "I never thought about it like that—like a lawman." She swallowed hard.

"It's too bad he got away." He clasped her still-trembling hand between his strong ones. The simple gesture comforted her, but his next words chilled her to the core.

"If Ojeda'd been caught, questioned and gone to trial, you would've been cleared—in the lawman's mind, if not in your father-in-law's. If Ojeda was smart, he headed straight for the border. From this part of New Mexico Territory, you have Oklahoma Territory and Texas both within a day's ride. He could be anywhere."

"Looking at it like a lawman"—she gulped—"if it weren't for the blizzard, the sheriff might've been ready to arrest me."

Jared shook his head. "He didn't sound like it to me. When I talked to him, I told him I was only investigating because the family was angry and upset over their son's death. He maintained it was unlikely you had anything to do with Ojeda killing your husband."

She let out a ragged sigh of relief. "You frightened me. For a moment, I was ready to make a run for Texas myself." While frontier justice was usually just, it wasn't always. Hanging a woman wasn't unheard of. Certainly not a frequent happenstance, but still... Her hand went to her throat.

"Already feeling the noose stretching your pretty little neck?" He chuckled.

"That's not even remotely humorous, Jared."

"Sorry, darlin'. Don't worry. You won't have to leave your land and hightail it to Mexico. If you want me to, I'll find Ojeda if I have to follow him to the ends of the earth."

"While I find your zeal immensely reassuring, I'd rather you not leave me."

"I don't want to leave you, Talia. Not ever." He put his hand to the back of her neck and pulled her down for a long and tender kiss.

Elation filled her heart. Her throat swelled with an unfamiliar emotion. Tears stung her eyes.

"What? What's wrong?" he asked her so tenderly she couldn't hold back the tears now coursing down her cheeks.

Shaking her head, she gazed down at him, unable to speak. Inhaling deeply, she composed herself enough to say, "I don't think I could bear it if you did."

"Then I won't."

"And tomorrow? You're still going to town?"

"Let's wait and see how the weather does."

She smiled, pleased that he'd put the decision off for another day. "If you go tomorrow, will you stop at Sarita's cabin and see if she made it home and if she and Pedro are all right? Their cabin is right off the trail to town, but still on the hacienda."

He nodded. "I will."

She laid her hand on his forehead. Beads of perspiration were just beginning to form. "Your fever is coming down," she said, then started to rise.

He clasped her wrist with his strong hand, forcing her to remain seated. "Don't go. Take a siesta with me."

"A siesta?" she said with a laugh. "What do you know about such things?"

"I know we could both use one."

"I know *you* need one, but I have other tasks to occupy my time."

"You don't have to see to the animals. I already did that."

"*Sí*, but I have to see to the house."

"Expecting company, are you?"

"You never know. In spite of your best efforts, my kitchen is in a sad state of affairs. What will Sarita say when she returns and sees the results of our, uh, cooking?"

His wide grin and the merry glint in his eyes sped up her heart. "By cooking, you mean the fact we just made love on the kitchen table?"

"*Dios*! She must never know." Natalia felt her neck and cheeks heat up hotter than the cookstove at dinnertime. "I must go."

Jared roared with laughter, but as soon as he stopped, his eyelids drooped with fatigue. "Whatever you say."

Placing a kiss on his forehead, she rose and rushed from the room. "Sleep, *mi amado*."

If she hadn't left the room when she did and allowed Jared to sleep off his fever, she would've lain beside him and run the risk of making his fever even worse.

Putting on an apron, she surveyed the remains of her kitchen. True, dishes were stacked neatly on the table by the sink, but there were fragments of broken crockery crunching beneath her boots. She and Jared had been so hot for each other that they'd swept everything off the table and hadn't even realized it.

Sarita would be appalled, even as she would be pleased Natalia had been so well loved. Tomorrow, if the weather allowed, she would remind Jared about checking on Sarita. Perhaps they would agree to shelter for the rest for the winter with her and Jared. Assuming, of course, Jared kept his word and didn't leave.

She set about restoring order to her kitchen, sweeping up the shards of crockery. After a futile attempt at using the water pump, she sighed. Still frozen. More snow would have to be brought in and heated to wash the remaining dishes and pans. Still, she couldn't help but be thankful for the storm that had marooned them together.

Once she had the snow melting on the stove, she dried her hands on her apron. Time to check on Jared. Hopefully by now, his fever had broken and he would've had a restorative nap. He might even still be asleep, and that suited her just fine, since anytime she was around him, she found herself unable to stay at arm's length. Indeed, she craved his strong arms around her as well as his masterful touch. It seemed he knew her body so well, what would pleasure her, even better than she. Making love with him was so natural, as if they were made for one another.

She tiptoed down the hall and stopped at the door to her bedroom. Hesitating, she laid her hand against the cool wood of the door. The chill from the surface sent a sensual thrill up her arm and then down to pool in her belly. Beyond this carved mesquite lay her beloved Pinkerton. How had they grown so close in such a short time? Never before would she have believed such a strong connection possible. Indeed, their bond was forged through adversity and shared dangers. But was it a lasting one, and would he truly stay with her after the snow cleared or the spring thaw, whichever came first?

After Reginald's death, she'd planned a future on her own as an independent woman. Marrying again had never entered her mind, but now, after all they'd been through, she looked forward to risking her heart for a future with Jared.

Fearing she might awaken him, she quietly turned the knob and nudged the door open until she could make out his form, stirring in sleep. Good, he was still resting. Ready to leave him undisturbed, she stepped back from the door but then heard him hoarsely call her name.

She opened the door wider and entered the room. "I thought—" She halted. Jared wasn't awake after all. He'd thrashed around and kicked off the coverlet. Swiftly, she crossed the room to his side, felt his forehead and found it damp with perspiration. His fever had broken, but why was he so restless?

"Jared," she murmured. Perhaps he was dreaming.

She started to ease from the room, but again he rasped her name. "Talia. I love you. Don't leave me."

Her heart thrilled to hear the words, even if only in his dreams. "I won't leave you, *mi amado*." As if she ever would. Reaching to caress his tanned cheek, she sighed.

Love for him overpowered her and filled her with a rush of emotions she'd long thought denied to someone like her—a woman bound in marriage to a man she hated. Her eyes stung with unshed tears.

His lids flickering, he grasped her hand, brought it to his mouth, and pressed light kisses into the palm. "Don't leave me."

"Never."

His eyes widened, his steely gaze locked with hers. "Do you mean that, Talia? Or are you playing with my feelings?" he asked her in a soft, seductive tone.

Assuming an offended expression, she straightened and jerked her hand from his. "You were pretending to be asleep—all this time? Shame on you, Pinkerton." Then she smiled. "Mayhap you were playing with my feelings instead."

Cocking a dark brow in her direction, he levered onto one elbow and grinned. "Knowing full well your fiery disposition, would I dare be so rash?"

"Cheeky fellow. I'll have you know most of the time I'm a very mild-mannered person." Natalia stood primly with hands folded while she endeavored to keep her expression meek.

"Except—"

"Except when I'm angry...or in bed."

"Yes." He nodded, with a smile playing about his tempting mouth. "Those would be the two exceptions I've noted."

"I believe the subject has been changed ever so subtly."

"It was a natural progression."

"I will never leave you, Jared. Can you truly say the

same?"

"Back to the topic at hand. When you choose to be, you're very direct."

"*Sí*, it pays to be direct when the stakes are high, Pinkerton. Yet again, you have avoided answering my question."

"Um, what was the question again?"

"Fine." Tired of playing Jared's silly game, she squared her shoulders. Ready to sweep from the room, she stopped only because he snatched her wrist.

"I will never leave you, Talia." Sitting up, he brought her hand to his heart and met her gaze. "I want to make my life here with you on this beautiful ranch where we'll have many children. Will you do me the great honor of becoming my wife?"

"Before or after the many children?" she asked, teasing him to cover her shock.

"Before, of course."

After Reginald was murdered, the last thing she ever wanted was another husband. He'd destroyed all her notions of what marriage should be. In her darkest hours, she'd sworn she'd never bind herself to another man. How things had changed in a few days, and it took only the love and attention of a good man. This good man.

"*Sí, mi amado*, I will marry you." Leaning forward, she cradled his face in her hands.

His eyes were warm and soft. "Come here. You're too far away." He scooted over and pulled her onto the bed beside him. "Lie with me, Talia." He gently stroked her cheek. "Let me make love to you for the rest of the night."

He drew her so close her head rested on his muscled

chest, and she could hear the hammering of his heart, even as her own raced along like a runaway horse. "*Sí*, love me for the rest of the night," she murmured.

Slowly, he peeled away the flannel shirt, revealing her breasts. The shock of cold air on her skin elicited a gasp. Her nipples tightened and tingled for more of his touch. He brought one of her breasts to his mouth. His tongue swirled languorously; then, centering on her nipple, he sucked. Need arrowed to her lower belly, causing her to whimper like a mewling babe. Never had she been treated so tenderly. Tears sprang to her eyes. She loved this man so. And now that he'd declared his love, he was hers for all time. "*Te amo. Te amo. Te amo.*" The words rushed from her lips like a sigh.

His rigid cock pressed into her thigh. He wanted her. He needed her as much as she needed him. She fumbled at the waistband of her trousers.

"Let me," he said. "I've had years of experience."

Nodding her assent, she smiled. "I suppose you have at that."

He rolled to his side and unbuttoned the fly of her pants, then slid them down her hips to her thighs. From there, she worked them below her knees and kicked them aside.

She gave an involuntary shiver at the room's cold air. His arms enveloped her as he pulled her to his warm chest. "Mm, better. Your body is warm as if you still have a fever."

"It's not the fever. I'm hot for you and your sweet loving." He pulled her close until her lower body covered his.

His cock jutted against her belly. More than anything,

she wanted to take him inside her and love him for as long as she could. "I don't want to hurt you."

"You're going to hurt me if we don't make love," she said, emitting ragged breaths.

She started to speak, but he shushed her. "There's no rush. We have all night." He cupped her buttocks, pressing his cock against her. She slid her hand between them and grasped him.

He gasped. "Easy, darlin'."

"I want you now. I don't want to wait." Natalia pushed off his chest and sat astride his hips. "Touch me. I'm wet for you. I'm ready."

He slipped two fingers into her cleft and groaned as her inner walls clenched around them. "If you're ready, so am I. He raised her hips, and she centered his cock at her entrance.

He tried to thrust home, but she shook her head. He groaned his frustration.

"Slowly, *mi amado*," she said, smiling down at him. Deliberately, she allowed his cock to enter an inch, then another, and another. Swirling her hips gently, she pulled away, then repeated the motion over and over until their bodies were straining for more contact. Moaning, he fisted his hands in the sheets as she took her time with their pleasure.

Finally, she took all of him, still squirming her hips to heighten the sensations. Then she began to ride him, at first slowly, then increasing the pace. He cupped her breasts as they bobbed, capturing one nipple between his teeth and raking it, causing curls of pleasure to weave their way through her body.

A rush of heat flooded through her as she rode him. She could never get enough of him...ever. His face flushed, the perspiration beading on his forehead as he strained upward, driving into her core.

Loving him, higher and higher she flew until her world exploded in a kaleidoscope of color. She collapsed in his embrace as he gave one final thrust and groaned.

Limply, her bones molten, she clung to him, gasping for air. "*Te amo.*" Amazingly she felt him stir within her.

He smiled up at her, his silver gaze blazing with heat. "Again, my love?"

"*Sí*, again. And again. And again."

Chapter Eighteen

The next morning, Jared hobbled out to the stables, leaving Talia still asleep in the bed they'd shared. The sun shone brilliantly on a vast expanse of white. Yesterday's wind had died down, and while the snow had drifted higher in some areas, the sides of the trench were merely knee-high. Finally, he could saddle his horse and forge his way the half mile to the housekeeper and her husband's cabin, if not all the way to town.

He quickly took care of feeding his restless stallion and Talia's gentle mare. Milking the cow wasn't his favorite task, but after last night's lusty exertions, Talia needed a brief respite from stable chores. He smiled at the memory of their loving. What a lucky bastard he was to have found a woman. Talia was his match in every way.

Back inside the ranch house, Jared set down a load of firewood, then grabbed a knife and cut himself a thick slice of bread. Chewing on the yeasty slice, he tiptoed into the bedroom. Talia still slept, her breathing regular and light.

Unwilling to wake her, he retreated to the kitchen, rummaged through the cabinet drawers until he found a pencil and quickly scratched out a note, telling her his plan for the morning. He left the note on the kitchen table where she would spy it. Soon they would know whether Sarita made it home through the storm to her husband.

Talia would be inconsolable if her housekeeper had perished.

He headed back to the stable, this time to saddle up. Today's temperature seemed mild compared to that of the previous day. Entering the stable, he heard the nickering of the horses. One of them pawed the ground restively. Midnight, no doubt. Yes. Midnight nodded his head excitedly, as if he sensed freedom was at hand.

Jared quickly bridled and saddled his horse, then led him through the stable door. Gritting his teeth against the pain in his injured leg, he set his left foot in the stirrup and carefully swung his bad leg over the horse's back. He nudged the horse forward with his heels, and soon they were making their way through the snow, around the side of the ranch house until they reached the front.

He could just make out the dip of the road. Midnight's muscles were tensed, ready to gallop, but the depth of the snow and the unfamiliar terrain kept Jared from allowing the stallion his head.

Still, he was a man with a mission. An uncompleted mission.

Behind him lay the ranch house and the woman he loved. Ahead lay the way to civilization, if indeed La Mesa, a town of two hundred or so, could be considered civilization.

In spite of the snow, Midnight appeared to relish the freedom, stepping high in order to move along. Jared kept a tight control on the reins. It wouldn't do any good to risk his mount by rushing along willy-nilly. The night before, Talia had told him where Sarita and her husband's cabin would be. In the distant northwest, he made out the snow-covered Rabbit Ear Mountains. Using those visible landmarks and the position of the sun, he guided his horse in a southwesterly direction.

A quick blast of air chilled his neck. He pulled his Stetson down, hunched his shoulders and continued toward the cabin. He could make out a bit of smoke coming from the chimney. Good. Someone was home...and alive.

As he rode closer to the cabin, he could tell someone had started digging out—just as he and Talia had. The area in front of the door was clear, and a partial trench had been dug. Anxious to reach the cabin, he allowed Midnight to move a little faster.

"That's far enough," a man's voice rang out.

Jared could make out that the cabin door was open, and the barrel of a pistol protruded. He stopped and raised his hands, showing he wasn't holding a weapon. "Pedro? *Señora* Montrose sent me. Is your wife with you?"

"*Sí. Mi esposa está muy enferma.*"

While Jared wasn't fluent in Spanish, he understood the gist of what Pedro'd said. Sarita was very ill. He pointed at the housekeeper's husband, then toward the hacienda. "*Vamos.*"

The pistol was lowered, and the door opened wider. A short, stocky man with a barrel chest stepped outside. "*Sí, señor.*" He then motioned for Jared to dismount and come inside.

Frowning, Jared nodded. Dismounting was a tricky proposition, since a normal dismount would bring his injured leg down first. Instead, he slipped his left foot from the stirrup, swung his bad leg over the horse's back, and slid off the horse. Not exactly an elegant maneuver, but at least he ended up with both feet on the ground. He hobbled forward, leading Midnight by the reins.

Too fast for Jared's limited Spanish, Pedro let fly with a rush of words.

"Hold on, *amigo*." Jared shook his head to let Sarita's husband know he didn't understand. He tied the horse's reins to the hitching post, the top of which was barely visible in the packed snow, and stepped into the small area Pedro had already cleared.

Jared gestured for Sarita's husband to enter first. The man nodded, and Jared followed. The strain of riding with his bad leg caused the muscles to cramp. There was a dying fire in the fireplace. In the corner lay Talia's housekeeper, covered in blankets and shivering. Her face was flushed, and her eyes were sunk back in her head. He'd never seen anyone who looked that bad who was still drawing breaths, ragged though they were. The way she coughed, she sounded like she might never breathe again.

If he didn't do something, the woman was a goner. "*Casa*," he said, jerking his thumb toward the ranch house. As cold as the ranch house was, they still had a good supply of firewood...and there was that supply of willow-bark tea Talia had used to save his own sorry hide.

Talia would know what to do if he could get her housekeeper back to the ranch house...if she could just survive the trip. The woman was in no condition to ride. He'd have to lay her across the saddle and lead Midnight back to the ranch. A half mile journey on his bad leg. He rubbed his thighs, willing the muscles to relax. No matter how much it hurt or worsened his injury, he had no choice. And best hurry, or Talia would lose her friend and housekeeper as surely as the sun rose each day.

Together, he and Pedro swathed the dying woman in wool blankets and carried her outside, then positioned her carefully over the saddle. "Go ahead," Jared said. "Tell *Señora* Montrose to prepare a bed. We're coming."

Pedro nodded and took off on foot, following the path Jared had created on Midnight. Apparently, Sarita's husband understood English better than he spoke it. Jared checked the woman's head, making sure it was wrapped against the cold. Untying the reins, he began the long, half-mile journey back to Talia—long only because of the snow and his injury; otherwise, the distance would've been nothing. "Let's go, fella," he said. The stallion nodded as if eager. They would follow Pedro as fast as possible.

He took a step and winced. No matter. He'd suffered worse pain in his life, and it would be worth the effort and pain if Sarita survived.

A loud banging startled Talia from a deep sleep. She sat and looked around for Jared. His side of the bed was cold, so he must've gone out to see after the animals. The banging kept up. It was coming from the front of the house. She swung her feet to the icy-cold tiles, grabbed the clothes she'd worn the night before and quickly dressed.

Who could be here pounding on her front door? Not Jared. He would've just come in through the kitchen. She ran to the front hallway, then opened the door.

"Pedro!" Her hand went to her throat. "What is it? Where's Sarita?"

"The *hombre*." He pointed over his shoulder and finished telling her how Sarita barely made it home through the blizzard and what had transpired since.

Trying to catch a glimpse of Jared, she peered over Pedro's shoulder. All she could see was a black speck...a very slow-moving black speck. She willed him to hurry.

"Build a fire in *el jefe*'s bedroom. While you do that, I'll saddle my horse and meet them. Jared's injured."

Pedro nodded and rushed away to bring in more wood.

It didn't take long for Natalia to saddle her mare and lead her around to the front of the hacienda. It seemed as if Jared and Sarita had barely moved since she first saw him over Pedro's shoulder. The pain in his leg must be excruciating from the cold.

Following the trail, she spurred Esperanza to increase her speed. The gentle mare obliged. As soon as Natalia reached Jared and the heavily bundled Sarita, she quickly dismounted and handed the mare's reins to Jared. "Here. You ride mine, and I'll lead yours."

"No."

"Don't argue with me. Switching up will save time. You're injured. You're in pain. I'm not. Now get back to the house and help Pedro get the fire going in Reginald's bedroom."

"But—"

"Go on. Get out of the way."

Shaking his head, he accepted the mare's reins and handed his to her. "Apparently, you're the boss," he said somewhat wryly, then mounted the mare and swung her head back toward the ranch house.

"Finally." She walked around Jared's stallion to check on Sarita. Pulling back one of the wool blankets, she discovered her housekeeper—no, her dear friend—was burning up with fever.

"*Santa Madre*." Her throat grew tight and her voice raspy.

Without another word, she began the trek back home. The stallion seemed to sense the urgency of their mission and picked up the pace.

She'd made the right decision in forcing Jared to ride back to the house on her mare. Sarita wouldn't have been in this condition if Natalia had been paying more attention to the weather instead of the very fine stranger in her parlor. There was no escaping the cold, hard fact: if her friend died, it would be Natalia's fault.

One step at a time, she slogged through the snow. Fortunately, today's wind was nothing like the first night's. She ducked her head and pulled her Stetson's brim down to shade her eyes from the sun's blinding glare on the snow surrounding her.

Once she was within yards of the front door, Jared and Pedro rushed out to meet her. The two men carefully pulled Sarita from the back of Jared's horse and together carried her inside.

Natalia had started to lead the horse back to the stable when Jared reemerged. "I'll take care of the horses." He jerked his head toward the open door. "Sarita needs you...and some of that tea."

She nodded and gladly surrendered the reins. Their hands lingered, touching for a second. Her heart swelled with gratitude. Her Pinkerton was truly a hero. "*Muchas gracias* for finding my friend." She ran for the door, then glanced over her shoulder. He raised his fingers to his mouth and blew a kiss.

For a brief second, his unfamiliar gesture startled her, but the meaning was as clear as the Rabbit Ear Mountains in spring. Pressing her fingers to her lips, she acknowledged the sentiment, then shot him a quick smile. Jared nodded and led the two horses away. In spite of Natalia's reluctance to see him go, she took a deep breath and told herself he wasn't going far and her friend needed her more than her lover. She waded through the knee-high drifts and slipped on an icy patch. Regaining her footing, she clung to the iron ring on the door, took another deep breath and went inside.

Once in the house, she threw off her heavy coat, leaving it where it fell, and rushed to Reginald's bedchamber. Pedro's quickly built fire was beginning to warm the room. Sarita lay buried under a thick pile of blankets and quilts. Her friend was shaking with hard chills and gasping with each breath. The woman's eyes were reddened and glazed with fever.

"Stay with her," she said to Pedro. "I'll fetch my store of medicinal herbs. We've got to get her fever down quickly."

Pedro nodded and moved from the fire to his wife's side. He dug under the blankets and pulled out her hand. "Hurry, *señora*. I was digging my way out to bring her to you when the *hombre*"—he angled his head toward the stables—"he came for us."

"He saved my life as well." She tugged on a corner of the covers to straighten them. "He's a good man to have around."

"*Sí.*"

With a quick nod, she rushed from the room. There was much to be done if she was to save her friend's life.

Chapter Nineteen

The next three days and nights passed in a blur. Natalia had never been so exhausted, not even when nursing Jared through his bout of fever. While Jared and Pedro took care of all the chores, including their meals, and had spelled her for brief rest periods, the stress of fighting to keep her friend alive had kept her awake.

On the morning of the fourth day, Sarita opened her eyes, and for once, they were clear. She looked around the room, her gaze widening when she appeared to realize where she was. "How...?"

Finally. Breathing a sigh of relief, Natalia eagerly clasped her friend's hand. "You've been ill. We brought you here."

"Pedro?" Sarita's gaze went around the room, searching. "How did he manage alone?" Concern crept into her tone. "The snow, it came down so fast. So deep. Is he all right?"

"Do not worry yourself. Pedro is with Jared—*Señor* Fields—in the stable. When the weather began to improve and the sun melted some of the snow, Jared rode over to your cabin."

Sarita pulled the coverlet to her chest, her fingers

picking at the material. "I was so sick I thought I was going to die."

Natalia swallowed the lump in her throat "For a time, so did I," she admitted, then plumped the pillows behind her friend's back, turning them over so the cooler surface would be next to Sarita's body

Natalia reached for the water pitcher and a cup. "Here. You need to drink something."

With a grunt, Sarita scooted up to her elbows, then finally to a sitting position. She grasped the cup in somewhat shaky hands and gulped.

"Easy," Natalia warned. "Not too much at one time."

Sarita sighed and nodded her understanding. Her eyes appeared brighter than they'd been in several days as she directed her gaze on Natalia. "How long have I been here?"

"Four days."

"That long?" Sarita asked. "You know, before I became so ill, I worried about you..." She cast Natalia a knowing glance, then continued. "But I was certain the gentleman would take care of you."

"*Sí*, he has." Natalia couldn't hide her smile. Indeed, Jared had taken excellent care of her. Likely she would've died without him.

"I thought for a moment I was dreaming," Sarita said. "Waking up here is almost like waking up in heaven."

"What good fortune we both had someone to take care of us." Natalia gave comforting pats to the back of her friend's hand.

"*Sí*. No matter how strong we both are, having someone at our side makes life worth living, no?"

"*Sí*." Natalia averted her gaze and set about

straightening the bed linens.

"Ah, from your simple answer and the expression on your face, I see that matters have progressed between you and *Señor* Fields. Or am I just a foolish old woman who merely hopes you have found someone, even if only for a time?"

"Foolish old woman—you? Never." Natalia crossed her hands over her heart. "I love Jared, and he says he loves me. Never wants to leave me."

"We women give our hearts easily, but men rarely do," Sarita said with a sudden frown creasing her forehead. "Are you so sure of this stranger?"

Was Sarita second-guessing herself? Somehow, Natalia had to convince her friend of Jared's worth. "He saved my life, *mi amiga*. He has shown me every consideration and been a helpmate. He makes love to me—unlike Reginald who used me for his basest needs. While it's true Jared and I have grown very close in a short time, our struggles to survive have forged a bond between us. As they say, we have weathered the storm. I simply cannot imagine the rest of my life without him."

"Tell me more of him—his background. What was his purpose in coming here, in the first place? Never forget you are a beautiful, rich widow, and there are unscrupulous men who wouldn't hesitate to take advantage."

Natalia laughed. "It's true, and I was suspicious of him...at first. He isn't after my money. No indeed, he was sent by Reginald's family to prove I'd had him killed."

Sarita's brows rose. "What?"

"*Sí*, he's a Pinkerton agent." She went on to tell Sarita of their ups and downs of the last week. The arguments. The struggles. "All that has changed. Jared loves me and wants to make his life here on the ranch. We'll have children." She crossed her hands over her abdomen. "We may already have made a child," she said with a smile. "Even if Jared were to leave me sometime in the future, he has already given me more in these few days than Reginald gave me in eight years."

"Then for that much, at least, I am thankful to *Señor* Fields." Sarita straightened, and her gaze shot toward the door. "I hear someone banging around in my kitchen." She struggled to lift the covers, then sank back into the pillows. "I must go..."

"No, you're still too weak to bother about the kitchen." In fact, Natalia hadn't seen the kitchen herself since bringing Sarita home. She could only imagine the disarray left by the two men.

"But—"

"But nothing. Jared and Pedro have taken over the household chores while I took care of you."

"You *let* those men in my kitchen? Are you *loco*?" Sarita let out a heavy sigh, then admitted, "Ah, well, I suppose it was the most reasonable division of labor, given the circumstances."

Natalia let out a laugh. "While their cooking isn't quite up to your standards, we haven't starved." No, indeed, they hadn't starved, but the men's cooking efforts were basically tamales and beans or beans and tamales.

"You think there might be something for me to eat?" Sarita's stomach growled, and she nodded vigorously. "See, I'm hungry—the best sign of all. I'm much better, even if I'm weak as a newborn calf."

A loud clang reverberated from the kitchen, accompanied by much swearing, then laughter. They must have returned from the stables already.

Sarita squeezed her eyes shut and covered her face with her hands. "*Dios mío*. What can they have done?"

"I'll go see." Natalia rose and started toward the door. "You'll be all right?" she asked over her shoulder.

Her friend nodded vigorously. "*Por favor*. See what those men are up to. It sounds like they are tearing it apart piece by piece."

"And having a good time doing it," Natalia said with a laugh and headed to the kitchen.

Jared stuck his burned finger in his mouth. When would he ever learn? He'd carelessly picked up the hot iron skillet of cornbread and promptly dropped it. The cornbread for their meal was scattered in yellow clumps all over the tiled floor.

"Just pulled from oven," Pedro said. "What you thinking? Never cook nothing before?"

Pulling himself upright and gathering what little dignity he had left, Jared gave an exasperated sigh. "Not before this week, no."

"*Hombre* has learning to do." Pedro snorted his disgust, bent over to pick up the cornbread, then stopped. "No, you do."

"Fine," he said, reaching for a broom. "I'm happy to clean up my own mess." In spite of Pedro's irascible nature, they'd become allies of a sort while Talia occupied herself nursing Pedro's wife. The man spoke more English than he initially admitted to and understood Jared quite well. Together they tended to the animals, and at night, they whiled away the hours talking beside the kitchen fire. By now, Pedro knew more about Jared's prior life than Talia did. His wild youth. Being disowned. Joining the Pinkertons as a last resort because the Pinkertons and peace officers were barely one step above the rat-catcher in the estimation of his former wealthy associates.

Most of all, Pedro knew of Jared's desire to give Talia more than his love and a strong back. He wanted to support her as a man should support his wife—financially— not live off her inherited wealth. Thus, he'd formed a plan. And if he had to go hat in hand to his father, he would.

"What's going on in here?" Talia rushed into the kitchen and stood with a very disapproving expression on her beautiful face. "You two have Sarita upset with all your noise and swearing."

"*Mi esposa*—awake?" Pedro straightened, his gaze darting toward the door.

"*Sí*," she said, smiling. "Go to her. I'll take care of all this." She gestured at the mess, then eyeballed Jared. "Or you will."

A wide smile spread across Pedro's face. "Can she eat something?"

"*Sí*, but not too much."

Pedro picked up a plate of eggs, then rushed to see his wife.

"I burned my hand again on that hot skillet," Jared said, hoping for a sympathetic response. "Perhaps there's some butter you could rub on it?"

Talia shook head. "I told you before. Ice for a burn. At

least that's what I think makes sense." She glanced at his hand and shrugged. "Not even a blister." She went to the back door, then turned to him with wide eyes. "The snow—it's almost gone."

"Yeah." He followed her and slipped his arms around her waist, pulling her close. Damn, but he'd missed her. "You haven't left Sarita's side in four days. I don't know how long the break in weather will last, but now that she's on the mend, I need to ride into town to the telegraph office and let my employers know how the situation stands." He'd waited longer than he should've, but he hadn't wanted to leave until Sarita was on the mend, in case Talia needed him.

"And your poor burned hand... Will you be able to manage the long ride?" Talia's expression was as sympathetic as could be, but her tone was decidedly amused. Humor glimmered in her black-olive eyes as she gazed upward. "And your leg—how has it fared these last four days?" This time her tone was a touch more serious.

"Not much pain." He shrugged. "But it still swells at night."

"Poor *bebé*," she said soothingly. "A rancher's life is hard. Are you sure you're up to the rigors of ranching?"

Jared squared his shoulders. "Never fear, *mi corazón*, I am ready to share your life, here on this ranch. Haven't we already been through more than one trial together?"

Her mouth curved into a smile. "*Sí*. I don't think I would have survived without you."

"You're a strong and determined woman, Talia. You would've survived." Grinning, he cocked his head to the side. "But it wouldn't have been as much fun as what we've had, though, would it?" He pulled her closer so there would be no doubt about how much he'd missed her. Needed her.

Her lips parted, inviting him to taste. And taste he did.

Her arms slipped around his neck as she clung to him. Four long days, she hadn't left her friend's bedside. And four long nights, he'd slept alone. And now he couldn't go another four seconds without having her.

He pulled her into the pantry, nudged her against the wall, lifted her skirt, and pulled down her underwear. Her hands grappled at the button closure of his trousers. He sucked in a quick breath when she touched him. Her fingers were cool on his cock as she pulled it free. Desperate to have her, he adjusted his stance and slipped a finger inside her cleft. Her inner muscles grasped his finger tightly as she gasped in his ear, "Quickly, before—"

He cut her off with his mouth and tongue, guided his cock to her entrance, thrusting inside with all the urgency of a man starved. Her silken pussy was hot and wet and enveloped him like a snug glove. Unable to hold back, he pounded into her, every nerve in his body on fire. An equal partner, she met and matched his intensity with every single stroke, her breath hot on his neck, as she shuddered against him, crying out as she came.

One more thrust and his world shattered. Gasping, crying, and laughing, they held on to each other until the world started turning again.

"Did we just do what I think we did?" she asked, smiling up, her eyes still glazed with passion.

"Definitely, we did."

Talia's cheeks were reddened from contact with his beard. Or was she blushing?

She bent over and pulled up her undergarments and straightened the folds of her skirt. "There. I'm presentable." She reached for his fly and started fumbling with the buttons.

"Let me do it. You'll just make matters worse," he said with a grin, then covered her slender fingers with his own and moved them to the side before unbuttoning his fly. "I'm embarrassed by my behavior, but I had to have you. Couldn't wait any longer." He caressed the silken skin of her cheek.

"Neither could I." She gazed at him, her eyes dark pools of sensual longing. "You didn't hurt your leg, I hope?"

"Leg's fine," he said with a casual shrug.

Her back straight, her attitude prim and proper, she walked back into the kitchen. Except for a slight flush, no one could know just a moment before he'd been buried inside her pussy, fucking against the wall, as if their lives depended on it, her body demanding all he could give, his cock wetly sliding in and out of her cleft. He shuddered at the memory and grasped the edge of the table to steady himself. God. He wanted her again.

"Perhaps I should clean up this mess before Sarita insists on viewing the damage for herself."

"What?" Still dazed from their heated encounter, he'd missed what she'd said.

Talia twirled around, her arms spread. "The kitchen—it's a disaster."

"Sorry about that. We tried...honestly."

"You said you needed to go into town, so why don't you do just that. I'll take care of this. Pedro won't want to leave Sarita's side now that she's awake. Oh, and while you're in town, find out what happened to the rest of my men and my two thousand head of cattle."

Giving a deep, theatrical bow, Jared grinned. "Would milady have any other tasks for this unworthy servant?"

"If you were truly my servant—unworthy or otherwise— you would've already cleaned up this kitchen." Reaching for an apron, she laughed and then tied it around her waist.

Unable to resist, he took a step toward her and spanned her waist with his hands. "As soon as I send a telegram off to my boss, I'll check on your ranch hands and the herd. And I'll see what the general store has to offer." In addition, he planned to stop by the sheriff's office and see if he had any news on Montrose's killer, Juan Ojeda.

Her arms snaked around his neck as she offered him her lips. He dipped his head and molded his body to hers. After a long, lingering kiss that threatened to keep him ranch-bound for the foreseeable future, she broke away gasping. "Now go, or I'll never restore Sarita's domain to its former glory."

"Woman, you're relentless, but I wouldn't have you any other way." He pulled her to him once more and kissed her forehead. "I'm off." He walked over to the coatrack beside the backdoor and pulled on his gear.

Chapter Twenty

The ride back to town was slow and torturous. Hampered by drifts and the unfamiliar terrain, Jared rode with care, his leg aching from the intense cold. At the signs of snow-covered roofs and smoke coming from more than one chimney, he let out a sigh of relief. He'd finally reached his destination. From all appearances, La Mesa had been hit hard by the blizzard, evidenced by the remains of the trenches which had been dug, leading from one business to another. Snow drifts were piled head-high in the walkways between the buildings that made up the small town.

Guiding his horse through the beaten, slick path in the middle of what passed for a street, he spied the sheriff's office on his right, across the street from the Silver Queen saloon. At the far end of town lay the railroad station, but it was too far to gauge any activity. Surely the sheriff would know about Talia's ranch hands and the status of her herd.

He aimed the horse's head to the trench that led to the local lawman's office and jail. Dismounting, he was careful to land on both feet. He tied the reins to the hitching post, stepped onto the wood walkway and knocked briefly before entering.

"Sheriff." Jared nodded.

Sheriff Moulton sat at his scarred desk on the right, reading the town's weekly newspaper. Moulton was a tall, gangly man with a beak of a nose and a sparse, grizzled beard. Directly across from the sheriff stood two jail cells. Only one was occupied. Jared's nose wrinkled. From the smell, the inhabitant was sleeping off a drunk.

Setting his paper aside, Moulton nodded back. "Wondered what mighta happened to ya, what with the blizzard and all."

"I managed all right." Jared shrugged and took a step forward.

"Notice you're a-limping."

"Yeah. Milk cow took exception to my technique and stepped on my leg."

The sheriff raised a quizzical brow. "Prob'ly a story behind that."

"Yeah."

"Whatcha need?"

"Couple things, Sheriff." Jared shifted his weight to his good leg. "Any news on Juan Ojeda?"

"Yeah. My deputy was out checking on folks and stumbled across him in a deserted cabin. Frozen stiff as a board."

"Have any large amounts of cash on him?" Even though he didn't for a single moment believe Talia was capable of hiring someone to kill her husband, he had to ask.

"Not one red cent. Reckon nobody paid him to kill Montrose, after all. Guess that takes care of your enquiry for his family."

"Reckon so." The weight on Jared's shoulders lifted.

Now he could keep his word to Talia.

"And the other thing?"

"Mrs. Montrose says when the storm hit, her ranch hands were ready to load up a herd of cattle. She's concerned about their welfare."

"Mrs. Montrose, huh?" Moulton tipped back in his chair, balancing precariously. "That where you 'managed all right' through the storm?"

"Yeah."

"Musta been rough—holed up in a blizzard with a purty widow like her." The sheriff's mouth twitched.

Jared held his tongue. No point in adding juice to the rumor mill.

"I hate to give the widow bad news, but the train never made it. We heard they'd been delayed by ice and snow over the tracks. And that was right before the telegraph lines went down."

"Lines still down? I need to notify my employer of the results of my investigation."

The sheriff shrugged. "Don't rightly know about the lines. As for her cattle, at least half of 'em froze to death or died of starvation. Her men hunkered down wherever they could. I'd check at the railway station. Some of 'em might be round there."

"Thanks, Sheriff. I'll do that."

Moulton nodded and went back to reading his newspaper.

At the telegraph office, Jared had quickly discovered the lines remained down. Thwarted in his desire to send his father a begging telegram, instead he left a message to be sent to Pinkertons as soon as the lines were operational. He turned, ready to leave, when the telegrapher stopped him. "Not so fast, mister. Got a telegram for ya. This 'un came right before the lines went down."

Jared took the missive and read it quickly, his heart dropping with the news. It was from his brother, brief and to the point. His father was dead of pneumonia and had been for a week. It also included a terse directive to come home and rejoin the family.

Now, still stunned by the news, Jared rode the two miles back to Talia's ranch. So much to consider. Obviously, his older brother wanted him to come home, take his rightful place, and stop living like a vagabond. As for his brother's suggestion that Jared stop acting like a ne'er-do-well—it wasn't an act. The label fit him as if he were born with it tattooed across his forehead.

After seeing the sheriff, Jared thought he'd have only the good news that Talia was cleared of her husband's death. While that was good news indeed and absolved him from any further responsibility to his employer, it was the only thing positive he had to relate. Over half of Talia's herd was dead, along with at least three of her cowhands, including her foreman, who hadn't been able to find sufficient shelter from the storm. Devastating losses all.

Down at the railway station, he'd seen an uncountable number of cattle frozen in place, now starting to thaw. If the weather continued to improve, the stench would be unimaginable. The sight of those dead cattle brought home the danger and rigors of life in northeastern New Mexico.

He and Talia could have died as easily as those

cowhands. Why risk everything on a piece of land when its continued success depended on a roll of the dice and the vagaries of nature? Now that his implacable father was dead and likely already buried, all he had to do was go home to New York and rejoin the family as if he'd never left.

Except for Talia. He couldn't leave her, not with her ranch in the midst of financial ruin. She needed him. But it was more than that. She was a part of him now, blood and bone.

But if she would leave the ranch and go with him to New York City, they could have good lives there, even if it wasn't what either of them expected. Until he talked with her, though, the future hung in a state of limbo. No need rushing to make a decision.

There was no getting around the fact that Talia's obstinate nature would be a major snag. But she had to understand her financial future was in jeopardy. If he could humble himself enough to return home and ask for another chance, then she wouldn't have to worry about the weather or an epidemic destroying her herd. True, she prized her independence and the land, but if she loved him as much as he loved her, she'd do it. She could sell what was left of her herd. The sale of the land alone would bring a sizable fortune which, under current laws, she would keep as her own, even after they married. All he had to do was swallow his pride and convince his brother of his maturity and willingness to work in the family business. Then he'd have the wherewithal to provide for a wife and family without touching her personal fortune.

There was no doubt about it, Talia wouldn't give in

easily; he'd have to be extra convincing. But having Talia at his side was worth the effort. The question still nagged him: did she love him enough to give up everything she held dear?

A gust of wind blasted through his coat, chilling him to the bone and almost ripping the Stetson from his head. Pulling up his collar, he hunched his shoulders and encouraged his horse to pick up some speed. Dark clouds in the northwest scudded across the sky, covering the dazzling sunlight. Maybe the storm had been a mere sampling of how bad the coming winter would be.

All the more reason to continue with his plan for taking her to New York.

Chapter Twenty-One

The hours crept by slowly. Once more, Natalia walked to the window, anxious for a glimpse of a certain horse and rider. The sun passed behind a bank of clouds, turning the vast field of snow a dull gray. A chill slid up Natalia's spine as she continued watching for Jared's return. Her hands clenched at her sides. What was taking him so long? What if his horse had lost its footing and Jared was lying injured somewhere along the road? Unbidden, her hand went to her mouth; she began to chew on one of her fingernails. Surely, he would return soon.

What if he never intended on coming back? What if his sweet words were all sugar and no substance. No. He was a better man than that. He would never treat her in such a dismissive manner.

The tromp of booted feet sounded behind her. She turned. Sarita's husband shifted from one foot to the other, his face pulled into a frown. "Pedro, is everything all right with Sarita?"

"*Sí.*" Pedro nodded vigorously. "*Mi esposa está más fuerte.*" He continued, telling Natalia how much Sarita wanted to get up.

Natalia frowned, then chewed her bottom lip while she considered. "She'll be very weak. Perhaps with your support, she could set her feet on the floor and take a step or two."

"*Sí, señora.*" With a wide smile, he nodded, then turned and rushed from the room.

She returned to her vigil at the window, wiping away the rime of frost which had appeared during her brief conversation with Sarita's husband. For a second, she thought there was no change in the landscape, but no, there was a small black dot on the horizon. It hadn't been there before. It had to be Jared. Clasping her hands to her mouth, she willed the dot to grow bigger until...

"*Sí!*" She could make out a horse and rider. It was Jared. A deep sigh of relief escaped her, leaving her still excited and nervous. Her lover had kept his word and returned. Resisting the urge to run and meet him, she hurried to a mirror. Who was the haggard creature staring back? Even though she'd cleaned the kitchen and then taken some care with her hurried ablutions, she was still a shadow of her former self. The days and nights of caring first for Jared and then for Sarita had taken its toll on her appearance.

Indeed, it was a wonder that he returned at all.

Pulling the pins from her hair, she raced to her bedroom. She grabbed a brush from the dressing table and raked it through the tangles. Once it was smooth, she took two ivory combs and slid them in at the temples. At least they would keep the stragglers off her face. She pulled the rest of it back and twisted it into a long curl, which she let drape over her shoulder. *Dios.* Her face was so pale. If she didn't know better, she'd think a corpse was peering back.

With a huff, she corrected her pallor by pinching her cheeks and biting her lips.

She straightened the collar of the flannel shirt she'd grown accustomed to wearing during the blizzard conditions. It would have to do until she had more time and energy to care about such nonessential fripperies as her appearance. When had she become so vain? Her late, unlamented husband had always demanded perfection in her appearance. As little as he cared about her, he made her very aware she was his possession and as such she represented him to the small world of La Mesa.

While Jared had never criticized her appearance, he was still a man. She wanted him to find her beautiful. And for once she was primping for a man because she wanted to, not because he made her.

Dreading to give Talia this heavy dose of bad news, Jared settled, fed and watered his horse in the stable before entering the house. His injured leg stabbed with pain every step he took, but again it was dread that slowed his pace more than pain. Underlying the dread, though, lay a degree of excitement and anticipation of what their future could possibly hold.

"Jared!"

Recognizing Talia's sweet voice, he glanced up. His breath caught in his throat at the sight of her standing at the kitchen door. God, she was beautiful. Even clad as she was against the cold in an ill-fitting man's shirt, her elegant beauty was undeniable and never failed to speed up his heart. He closed the distance between them and swept her into his arms. Burying his face in her hair, he breathed in her unique scent. She eased her arms around his waist as she pulled him inside the house.

"What a welcome," he said with a laugh. "You must've missed me."

"Indeed I did, Pinkerton. I'd begun to despair of ever seeing you again." She finished this statement with a lovely, low laugh that resonated through every cell in his body. But the bad tidings he had yet to reveal dampened his ardor.

She reacted immediately. "What's wrong? You've stiffened up on me."

"That's supposed to be a good thing," he said in an attempt to lighten the mood.

"You know very well what I mean. You're tense." Still in his arms, she pulled back, her unerring gaze seeking the truth in his. Dark as ebony, her eyes bore through to his soul. "Tell me. Tell me now—this bad news you seek to hide."

He clenched his jaw, then said, "Let's go into the drawing room where we can sit. My leg's aching from the cold. Feels like it's been caught in a bear trap."

His words diverted her from his bad news, and her expression grew concerned. "I'm sorry. I wasn't thinking. Of course you need to sit."

Together they walked into the drawing room, her arm around his waist. She took her spot on the settee and patted the cushion beside her. "Now sit. You can't put me off any longer."

Reluctantly, he sat and stretched out his bad leg, hoping to relieve the muscle spasms. "Three of your men didn't make it, including your foreman."

Talia's chin dropped, trembled, and her bottom lip quivered. "*Madre de Dios.*"

"The railway stationer said most of the others found shelter, but those three didn't make it. They tried to care for the herd."

"What about the herd? Surely the train...?"

"The train didn't make it. Over half your herd's gone."

She paled. He watched the muscles in her throat work as she tried to swallow. Her trembling hand went to her mouth. "Gone?" she gasped.

"The rails were blocked by snow drifts. The telegraph lines went down, but they're already working on getting those back up."

"La Mesa is shut off from everything?"

"For now. If the weather continues to improve, we may still get the rest of your herd to market."

"It's a disaster to be sure, financially, but those three men..." Her gaze grew inward as she chewed on her knuckle.

"Did many of the men have families?"

She shook her head. "No—at least not locally. Some of them may have family back East. I do know my foreman has a wife and four children in St. Louis, although only one child is still at home. He was saving every penny he made, since he intended to bring them out here next spring. I'll have to let them know. I need to make arrangements. See to their welfare or bring them out here as he would've wanted."

"Yes, we'll see that they're cared for."

That was the second time Jared used the word we. He

meant it too.

Talia gazed at him, gratitude lighting her eyes. "I'm so glad you're here. I know I've said it many times, but I don't know what I'd do without you."

"You won't ever have to find out," he said, mentally re-reading the telegram still in his coat pocket. Should he risk testing the depth of her love or not? She never needed to know about his brother's offer. All he had to do as soon as the lines were back up was wire his brother with a polite "Thanks, but no thanks". But doing so wouldn't solve Talia's financial problems or allow him to support her instead of the other way around.

"We'll get through this together, Talia."

"I truly believe we can." She grasped his wrists with her long, elegant fingers. Raising his work-hardened hands to her mouth, she kissed each knuckle. "Did you see the sheriff? Is he going to arrest me?" she asked carefully.

"Moulton told me that Ojeda had hidden out in a deserted cabin. Dead from the cold. And he didn't have one red cent on him, which we both took to mean no one paid him to kill your husband. As far as the sheriff and I are concerned, you're officially cleared of his murder."

Her mouth pulled into a somewhat guarded smile. "And now I trust you'll communicate that to the Montrose family."

"You bet your sweet lips. In fact, I left a message to be sent as soon as the telegraph wires are repaired."

"Will they be satisfied?" she asked.

"Whether or not they'll be satisfied, I doubt it. But there's nothing they can do if the sheriff says you're in the clear."

"Your assignment here is complete. You could leave." Her tone was calm, but he detected a slight quaver.

He took her hands in his. "I said I would never leave you, and I meant it."

"But what about Pinkerton's?" She kept her gaze averted as if fearing his response. "Won't they mind?"

"Talia, I was a Pinkerton employee, not their indentured slave. When the wire about Ojeda goes through, it also contains my resignation. "

Her warm gaze met his. "Is it really that simple? You just send a telegram saying you're through?"

He nodded. "Just that simple."

True, resigning was easy enough, though the pull of loyalty to the organization which had given him a new start was strong. Only his love for Talia could have induced him to resign.

On the other hand, his brother's telegram was another deal entirely. The call of family was ever-present. It wasn't his father's death that disturbed him so much as the thought of a reunion with his brother and what was left of their family. It'd been over ten years since he'd graced the family home. Since being disowned, he and his brother hadn't been close. Perhaps too much time had passed. Could they really make a life in New York? How in hell could he convince Talia to move when he had so many doubts?

Black sheep. Wastrel. No-good. Those were some of the names his father labeled him with. Too bad he couldn't prove the old man wrong. Maybe—no, not maybe—the names had fit Jared ten years ago when he'd gambled away his mother's inheritance without a second thought. But he was a man now. And while the lure of cards and dice might still plague him on occasion, his power to resist was stronger, especially now that the stakes were so high.

"What's wrong? There's more?" Her cool hand trembled. She pleaded with her eyes for him to tell her she was mistaken.

Better to tell her now than later. He cleared his throat, stalling for the right words. "Before the lines went down, I had a telegram from my brother telling me my father passed away a week ago."

Her dark gaze softened as she spoke. "I'm so sorry, but he wasn't good to you, was he?"

"No. But then I wasn't a very good son most of the time." *Hard-headed, strong-willed*—more names his father called him.

"No!" Her hands clenched in front of her. "He was cruel to you when you were a child."

Jared's breath caught in his throat. He could barely utter the words, "How could you possibly know?"

He watched as she took a deep breath and then let it out, her full breasts rising and falling with the effort. "The fever—you ranted a bit—enough for me to understand what your childhood must've been like." She caressed the back of his hand as if she could wash away all his pain. "It broke my heart to hear you, and I comforted you the best I could."

Never dreaming she knew so much about his early life, Jared clenched his jaw. She'd seen him at his weakest and most vulnerable and never let on until now. He watched for the inevitable pity to appear in her expression.

"You're a wonderful man, Jared. The past may influence

who we are now, but the future is more important. Our future, if that is what you desire."

There was no sign of pity in her warm gaze. Instead, he saw acceptance and, yes, love. Still, his old doubts nagged him. Was it enough love that she'd abandon the only life she'd ever known?

He covered her hands with his. "There's more."

"More?"

"My brother wants me to return to the bosom of the family, so to speak."

She straightened and raised her chin. "Then you must go. Your family needs you." Again there was the slightest quaver in her voice.

Setting his hands on her shoulders, he pleaded his case. "Come with me. I'll take my place in the family business. I'll be able to support *you*. We can have a fabulous life in New York. We'll have money, a luxurious home. You won't have to worry about blizzards and the price of cattle. As for the herd—sell what's left. Sell the land too. That'll give you a small fortune for your personal use."

"Stop!" Talia covered her ears. "I've heard enough." Her eyes blazed. "How dare you? Sell my land, the land for which I suffered eight long—and I must add miserable—years. This land is *mine*. I'll never give it up. Haven't you been listening? I thought you understood me, but if this is your facile solution to my problems, you're not the man I thought you were. Not at all. Cattle ranching is difficult in the best of times, and if you're not willing to stand beside me, we don't have a future."

Each furious utterance slammed Jared like blows to the gut. Worse, because it demonstrated how little she thought of him and his desire to support her as any man worth his salt would. As he'd feared, she just didn't love him enough.

He reached for her and clasped her in his arms. "Talia," he began, "you have it all wrong. I need to be more than your glorified ranch hand. I want to support you on my own terms—financially. And I can't do that unless I return to New York. I don't know the terms of my father's will. There may or may not be anything for me, but reading between the lines of my brother's telegram, I'm sure I can make a good life for us there."

"I've never cared about luxury or a place in society." She gave her head a furious shake. "I've already had one husband who treated me like a piece of the furniture. Marriage to Reginald was all for show. Never a true partnership. But somehow I fooled myself into thinking you were different." Her eyes shining with unshed tears, she pulled away. "I can't believe I was ready to give up my independence for you. You, a man who can't weather a little snow."

Damn, it was going all wrong. Better he should try a different approach. "It's not the weather or the hardships. I thought you loved me, and anywhere I was, you'd want to be."

"You, Jared. I wanted *you*." Her voice broke as if she could barely get the words out. "I didn't care if you were the son of a rich man or a farmer. I wanted you at my side. I wanted to have your children. Damn it, I would've signed the land over to you. We would've been full partners."

Jared shook his head. "I wouldn't let you do that. This is *your* land, Talia. You're damned straight you've earned it. I don't care about the hardships. After the last week, we've proved we can get through anything. But can you blame a man—a real man, because you obviously weren't married to one—for wanting to support his wife?"

Rising to her feet, she gazed down at him in disbelief. "So selling and moving to New York is about your male pride?"

"Yes...what little I have left." He shifted his leg, hating to admit how pathetic he sounded. "Before I received the news of my father's death, I was going to humble myself and ask him for the money to rebuild the herd and save your ranch."

"After he was so unkind, you would've done that for me?" Tears glimmered in her dusky eyes, then started trickling down her cheeks. She sniffed and wiped the moisture away with the back of her hand.

"I would," he said simply, although in reality, swallowing his pride wouldn't have been easy. He stood to face her.

"And now? Will you still return to your family?" She stepped closer, sliding her arms around his waist and resting her head on his chest. "Wouldn't you at least like to see your brother—for a visit?"

Unbelievably, she seemed able to read his mind as if she knew him better than he knew himself. He shook his head. "Not now. Not without you, Talia. And if you allow me to stay, to be your partner, then there's too much work to do with the ranch. We have to rebuild your herd—"

She caressed his cheek. "*Mi amado*, we could have the rest of our lives."

"Do you mean it?"

"*Sí*, with all my heart."

"Talia, will you still marry me, such as I am? All I may ever have is my vow to love you until I draw my last breath."

"*Sí*, Jared, I have not changed my mind. I will marry you. All that matters is that we face life together. I love you so much...even more than my land."

"More than your land?" Jared let out a sharp bark of laughter. "That's saying something. 'Cause I know how you love this land, this ranch."

"But I warn you. I'm not an easy woman be around. "

"You're easy to *love*," he said, drawing her close. "No other woman has ever made me feel what I feel when I'm with you. It doesn't matter if we're mucking out the stable or making love on the kitchen table..."

"I had no idea you were such a poet," she said with a quiet laugh, putting her fingers to his lips. "Shh, you must *never* let Sarita know. You promise?"

"I promise," he said with a smile. "Our secret forever." Clasping her hands, he swung her around. "Now, let's go tell Sarita and Pedro—"

"You promised!"

"—our good news," he finished with a smile. "Silly woman."

Epilogue

The late July sun beat down on Natalia while she watched Sarita gathering herbs from the small garden at the back of the patio. New cattle were grazing on the distant hills, while horses trotted around the pasture. After the unceasing cold of the last winter, the heat was welcome indeed. She rubbed her huge belly, wishing the nagging twinges she'd experienced all day would go away. She shifted uncomfortably on the wrought-iron chair. *Dios!* Now her back was aching as well.

Unthinking, she let out a loud sigh. Sarita's head turned sharply in Natalia's direction. "Is it the *bebé*?"

"No, but now my back is aching." Without warning, a rush of warm fluid gushed between her thighs and spattered on the patio tile. "I'm all wet." She rose clumsily from the chair, clutching the table to steady herself. A sharp cramp started in the middle of her back, circled to each side, then met in the middle of her belly. The sharp pain arrowed down to her lower belly.

Sarita straightened. "It *is* the *bebé*."

"No, not yet. Jared's in town. He won't be back in time."

"Oh, he has plenty of time," Sarita said chuckling. "The

first one is always the longest. You'll see." She slid her arm around Natalia's waist. "Let's get you into a clean gown and into the bed."

"Where would I be without you, Sarita? You've always been here for me. A mother could've done no more than you have." Tears started flowing down Natalia's cheeks. "Why am I crying? What's wrong with me?"

"Nothing wrong with you. You're having your *bebé.* Either a fine son like his *papi* or a beautiful daughter like her *mami.*"

"I want Jared. I want him here."

"He will be. Never fear."

Once inside her bedchamber, Natalia allowed her lifelong friend to remove the wet skirt and slip a fine cotton shift over her head. She lay down, sinking into the soft feather mattress with a sigh.

Then the next pain hit, harder than any before, and her real labor began.

The keening sound knifed through Jared's heart. Every pang Natalia suffered, he suffered. He sat at the kitchen table, staring unseeingly at his pocket watch. "How long has it been?" he asked Pedro, who merely poured another shot of whiskey and handed it to him.

Jared snapped the fob shut. "Useless. I'm so useless."

Another gut-wrenching scream emanated from their bedroom.

"I can't stand it. She sounds like she's dying. She needs me." He couldn't lose her now. Not after all the struggles of the hardest winter he'd ever known. They'd married in the early spring, and he'd rejoiced when she told him she was with child. His child. He couldn't lose her now. It wasn't fair.

"Drink up, *amigo*. She doesn't need you. Doesn't want you to see her like that." He shook his grizzled head. "This is women's work."

"I never thought it would be this bad. Women have had children for centuries. Why on earth would they go through pain like this?"

"For love, *mi amigo*. For family." Pedro shrugged. "Women have the *bebés*, and men work to support them. That's life."

Jared downed the whiskey. Fine. Pedro could be as philosophical as he pleased, but it wasn't *his* wife in agony two rooms away.

A scream—primal—unlike any he'd heard before tore him from his seat. "My God, it's killing her!" Unsteadily, he got to his feet.

Then a squall sounded through the air. Angry, furious, and the most glorious sound Jared had ever heard. His knees weakened. Grabbing the table, where they might've actually conceived their baby, he sagged into the chair. The room swam before his eyes. All he could see were alternating splotches of green and black. He struggled to see his drinking partner.

"Head down, *amigo*," Pedro ordered. "Between your knees."

Though it made no sense, Jared complied. "Wha—"

"'Bout to pass out." The man chortled. "*Sí.*"

With blood once again going to his head, Jared's vision cleared, but he was still dizzier than he'd ever been in his entire life. "Glad you find me so amusing, *a-mi-go.*"

"They won't let you in there until you can stand on your feet. Wouldn't want to drop your *bebé*, now would you?"

"My baby?" He stood again, this time steadier. "My God. I have a baby." Without waiting, Jared rushed toward their bedroom. The door was still closed. He hesitated for a moment, then tapped.

The door was opened immediately. "What took you so long, *señor*?" Sarita ask. "Your *bebé* and your wife, they are waiting for you." She stepped back, and finally he could see the woman who meant everything to him. Tired but beautiful beyond his imagining, she smiled up at him, their baby bundled in the curve of her arms.

"I thought you were dying," he said. "I wanted to die with you."

"Don't be silly. Are you ready to meet your"—a playful smile lit her face as she kissed the top of their baby's head—"son?"

"A son? We have a son?"

"*Sí*. He's long. He'll be tall and handsome like you one day. And I hope he'll be as wonderful a man as his father." She kissed their baby again. His son would grow up with love and an adoring mother and father. "What shall we name him?"

He smiled down at his wife and son. "Over the last couple of weeks, I've been giving the name some thought. Now that my brother and I have resolved our issues over Father's estate, I thought we might name him Garth—if that's all right with you."

Talia smiled and finger-combed the baby's dark thatch of hair. "Well, little *Señor* Garth Fields, this is your father." She glanced up. "Don't you want to hold him?"

Still a little shaky, Jared played it safe and sat on the

bed beside his wife. His hands shook as Talia passed the small, squirming bundle into his arms. His heart thundered. His child. Their child. To love and care for the rest of their lives.

"Support his head," she warned.

He nodded, still unsteady.

Over by the door, a smiling Sarita stood wrapped in Pedro's arms. Apparently his drinking partner had carried tales and told her of Jared's nearly passing out.

"Are you happy?" he asked the mother of his child.

Talia gazed up at him, the love shining in her eyes. "I've never been so happy." She reached up and caressed his cheek, causing his heart to swell with love.

"Neither have I. And this is only the beginning." Luckiest man in the world couldn't begin to describe how he felt. He had everything a man could ever want. A home, a beautiful and passionate wife, and now this precious babe.

The End

Author's Note

For anyone who wonders about the suddenness of the blizzard in the story, there really was a severe snowstorm in late October 1889. And according to reports of the time, it came without warning. The real storm was even more severe and tragic than depicted in this story in that there were no thawing winds from the southwest.

Bonus Material

Please enjoy this excerpt from the next book in this series, MASTERING THE MARSHAL.

US Marshal Sam Dunaway tied his horse to the hitching post in front of the sheriff's office and surveyed the small town of Kenton Valley. Typical of most small Texas towns, it had a church, a general store, dry goods, and two saloons. Down at the far end of the street was a school, where he heard the excited shouts of children playing some game or other.

He brushed the fine yellow dust from his oilskin duster and was ready to step onto the walk when a scrawny, redheaded boy ran up.

"Marshal! Are ya a-going to hang that feller what shot the sheriff's missus?"

He gave the boy his sternest expression. "Not without a trial first."

"He's guilty. Ever'body says so. I wanna see him swing."

So young and so bloodthirsty. Sam shook his head. "I suspect your mama will keep you home that day. If you were mine, I would."

The boy shifted from one foot to the other. "Dang it. Hey, I'm gonna be a lawman when
I grow up."

"That's mighty fine, kid. Say, what's your name?"

The kid puffed out his chest. "William Robert

Rasmussen, but folks call me Billy."

"Well, Billy, being a lawman is a tough job. Need to be smart—"

"And fast with a gun." The kid did an imaginary quick draw.

"Being smart's more important." Sam hunkered down to the boy's level. "How come you aren't in school?"

Billy screwed his face into a frown. "School's stupid."

"Not so. If you want to be a lawman, you gotta go to school. That's all there is to it."

"Really?" His eyes widened in surprise.

"Really. Now go on. Git."

Shaking his head, Sam stood and watched until he was sure the boy had reached the end of the street. Damnation. What was it with kids today? In a hell of a hurry to grow up, when these were the best times of their lives.

He opened the door to the sheriff's office and nodded. "Sheriff Cordero Tate?"

The sheriff nodded. "Cord'll do." The sheriff was tall and broad-shouldered and showed no signs of his prior tragedy. He rose and offered his hand.

Sam took it. "I'd like to see the prisoner and how he's housed."

Tate stood and opened the door leading off the main room. It led to a cellblock, containing two cells. Only one was occupied. Barnes was stretched out, apparently asleep on the bunk-as if in a few days he wouldn't be sleeping forever.

Sam turned and walked back to the outer office. "Appears you have a sturdy enough jail. Any chance the rest of his gang might try and break him out?"

"I've got two trustworthy deputies. Besides"-the sheriff

shook his head-"the gang's ringleader was killed last summer. The rest of 'em splintered after that. 'Course, you never know." He shrugged. "Catching Barnes here was more of an accident than anything. He couldn't resist visiting his sick mama. Thought he might show up, so we took turns keeping an eye on the Barnes homestead."

"Smart thinking. If I'm not mistaken, you're the one who killed the ringleader, Tyler?" Not to mention the sheriff's new wife was Tyler's half-sister. Wonder that didn't complicate things.

"That's right." Tate sat, gesturing for Sam to pull up a chair.

A man of few words. Good. Removing his Stetson, Sam hooked the toe of his boot around a chair leg, dragged it over and straddled it. Now they could get down to the business of the trial. "I need a place to hold the trial. Any suggestions?"

"Haven't had much call for trials till now. There's the school or the church or the saloon."

"Good. I'll check 'em out. Prefer a neutral ground over the saloon. Any chance we'll find twelve sober men come trial time?

Tate shrugged. "If you'd rather move the trial to a bigger town, it won't hurt my feelings none."

Sam shook his head. "I'm here to see he gets one. Don't care if it's fair or not. That's up to the judge, not me." He stood and settled the Stetson on his head. I'll head over to the church, then to the school. Let you know which one I decide."

The sheriff nodded. "Any word on when the judge will get here?"

"Few days. He's presiding over a trial in Llano." Sam

headed to the door, then stopped. "The livery?"

"Livery stables are behind the boarding house at the north end of town. Miz Foley oughta be able to fix you up while you're here." Tate jerked his head in the direction of the cells. "She provides meals for the prisoner, and she's a damn fine cook."

Sam touched the brim of his hat, nodding his appreciation.

Outside, he untied and mounted his horse, then headed north, passing the general store and dry goods. He glimpsed the tall, slender figure of a woman standing in the window of the dry goods store, a sudden apparition that had him twisting around in his saddle to get a better look. But his horse had other ideas and kept heading north.

Damn. She looked familiar, so familiar his heart sped up and his mouth went dry as sand. Just the memory of their loving stiffened his prick. But it couldn't be Celine. His wife had burned to death in a boardinghouse fire near-on three years ago.

When the news of her death had finally reached him, he'd still been too angry to grieve. She never would've died if she'd stayed home where she belonged instead of running off with his life savings. Served the bitch right— that was what he'd thought at the time.

But now... If this woman really was Celine and not someone who was her spitting image, what he wouldn't give to bed his wife one last time before he locked up the thieving bitch.

About the Author

Marie-Nicole Ryan grew up in western Kentucky, and after living for several decades in Nashville, TN, she returned to her old stomping grounds in Western Kentucky. Before she gave up her glamorous day job to write fulltime, she was an RN case manager.

She's an award winning erotic romantic suspense author and a former member of ROMANCE WRITERS OF AMERICA® and MUSIC CITY ROMANCE WRITERS.

She lives with a Sheltie rescue by the name of Kelsea who, if she could talk, would no doubt have amazing stories of her own to tell.

You may find more about her work at the following sites:

Web site: https://marienicoleryan.com
Facebook: https://facebook.com/marienicoleryan.author
Twitter: @marienicoleryan
eMail: marie@marienicoleryan.com